What dreams may die
CF Ter Sweet #3

T50237

DISCARDED

9/19

Help us Rate this book...
Put your initials on the
Left side and your rating
on the right side.
1 = Didn't care for
2 = It was O.K.
3 = It was <u>great</u>

	DATE DUE		
OCT 2 1 2019			
DEC 0 7 2019			
DEC 2 6 2019			

1 2 3
1 2 3
1 2 3
1 2 3
1 2 3
1 2 3
1 2 3
1 2 3
1 2 3
1 2 3
1 2 3
1 2 3
1 2 3
1 2 3

DISCARDED

PRINTED IN U.S.A.

" 'What no eye has seen, what no ear has heard, and what no human mind has conceived' — the things God has prepared for those who love him."
1 Corinthians 2:9

Note: The views of the characters in this novel do not necessarily reflect the views of the author, nor is their behavior necessarily being condoned.

What Dreams May Die
Copyright © 2018 Alana Terry
February, 2018

Cover design by Cover Mint Designs.

www.alanaterry.com

CHAPTER 1

Megan reached up to hug her brother. "It's great to see you. I'm still so sorry I missed your wedding."

"You can stop apologizing." Scott plucked her suitcase out of her hand and tossed it into the backseat of his car. "How was your flight? Everything go okay?"

She nodded and tried to hide her yawn. "Everything was fine. But I'm ready to hide away from the Costa Rican heat for a while."

"Well, don't get your hopes up. Orchard Grove's been in the nineties every day for the past week." Scott gave her one more hug. "I'm so glad to see you. The last time we were together you were still crying over that jerk who ..."

"It's been a long time, hasn't it?" she interrupted. She stopped herself from apologizing one more time for not being able to fly out to Orchard Grove when he and Susannah got married last winter. Megan sat beside her brother and buckled up.

Scott hadn't stopped grinning since baggage claim. "Are you hungry? We could grab something for the road."

"Starving."

"You in the mood for anything in particular?"

Megan paused to think. "Anything that's not a legume." She never knew until moving to Costa Rica to work with Kingdom Builders how black beans could turn into breakfast, lunch, and dinner staples. Her taste buds were ready for a nice, juicy burger or greasy slice of pizza. This felt just like it had when she was a teenager and spent her spring break with Scott while he was getting his Bible certificate. Just the two of them, together again.

Except now he was married and about to become a father. "How's Susannah?" she asked as they pulled away from the curb.

Scott maneuvered through the congested airport traffic. "She's adorable. Like always. Being pregnant hasn't slowed her down a bit."

"And what about her sister?" Megan asked. "How's Kitty doing?"

She glanced over at her brother and for the first time saw his smile diminish.

"She's hanging in there," Scott answered. "She's one tough cookie, that's for sure."

"Well, I'm excited for the chance to get to know her." Megan didn't want to admit she was nervous. Not about meeting Scott's wife. She and Susannah had shared plenty of phone calls and video chats, and Megan had heard enough about Susannah from her brother that she felt like they had known each other for years.

What she was less certain about was Kitty, Susannah's sister who had cerebral palsy and was recovering from pneumonia. Scott had tried to sugar-coat Kitty's recent sickness on the phone. That was just his way, but Megan knew her brother well enough to suspect that things weren't as optimistic as he made them out to be.

Which was one of the main reasons Megan had flown all the way to Washington state to be with her brother and sister-in-law. Susannah could use the extra hands around the house, especially now that she was pregnant in addition to taking care of her sister. Megan was past due for a furlough anyway. Most of the other missionary teachers at the Kingdom Builders school and orphanage left Costa Rica once every year or two, but Megan had stayed on the field over four years straight.

So much had changed since then.

"I still can't believe you're about to become a dad." Megan winced when she said the words. Scott would be a great father. She knew that with certainty, but she still couldn't picture him settled down with a family of his own.

Would there still be room left in his heart for her?

He looked just as casual and at ease as ever. "Well, I'm sure you had a long day. Feel free to take a little nap. We can stop by Zips for some food on our way out of town."

Megan leaned back in her seat. There were so many things she wanted to ask her brother. How did he end up falling in love with Susannah before they'd even met face to face? Was it hard sharing his home with a sister with disabilities? Had it been a difficult choice to give up his frequent mission trips with Kingdom Builders to settle down?

Did he ever regret his decision, even a little?

But there would be time for all that later. Megan wouldn't be heading back to Costa Rica until September. It was a much-needed break after four and a half long years on the field.

Scott knew more than anyone how difficult her first few months had been. Eventually the two of them would end up talking about all of it, but for now she just enjoyed his nearness. She rolled down her window, sighing as the wind whipped through her hair.

She'd never set foot in Washington state until now, but still it felt good to be home.

CHAPTER 2

"It's so nice to finally meet you." Megan accepted Susannah's hug and hoped she didn't smell as gross as she felt after a full day of traveling. It was a two-hour ride by bus from the mission complex to the San Jose airport, and she was covered in dust and sweat. Thankfully, Scott and Susannah's home had air-conditioning. She could definitely get used to this.

Megan pulled away and studied her sister-in-law. "You don't even look pregnant!"

Susannah laughed easily. "Four months along already."

Scott beamed and rubbed his wife's belly. "If you go by the pregnancy calendar, our little baby's about the size of an orange and growing bigger every day." He leaned down and let his voice rise an octave. "Aren't you, little baby? You're growing so big for your mommy and daddy who love you so much."

Megan had never seen her brother baby-talk to anyone before. She wondered what her parents would think, then shoved the thought away. "How's Kitty doing?"

Susannah's smile wavered for just a second. "She just woke up from her nap. She's looking forward to meeting you." Why did she look so nervous?

Megan glanced at her brother.

"Kitty can sometimes take a little time to decide if she likes you or not," Scott whispered while his wife headed down the hall.

"Is everything okay?" Megan still wasn't exactly sure how she was supposed to act around someone with cerebral palsy. Kitty couldn't talk, but she used other cues to communicate. Megan was afraid she'd forget the difference between one kick and two or find some other way to accidentally insult Scott's new family.

"Kitty," Susannah was calling from the doorway. "Are you ready to meet Scott's sister? Megan's here all the way from Costa Rica. Remember how much we pray for her and her work with the orphans there?"

Megan glanced up once more at her brother. Was she supposed to head down the hall now or wait to be invited? Funny how she could handle a classroom of forty rambunctious students, preaching Bible stories and teaching multiplication facts in a second language, but now that she was back with Scott, she reverted so readily to her old role.

The role of the little sister in need of protection.

The attention-starved child looking to her larger-than-life brother for reassurance.

Or the heartbroken new missionary crying on her brother's shoulder her first Christmas on the field.

"Go ahead," Scott whispered. His smile was warm and kind. Maybe they were both falling back to old roles.

Scott took her arm and led her down the hall. "Oh, Kitty," he called out in a sing-song voice. "Guess who's here to see you? You ready to meet your new sister?"

CHAPTER 3

Brad's mother was already crying before he pulled away from his first hug.

"It's okay, Mom," he told her. "I'm here. You can let me go now."

"I'm just happy to have you back home." She sobbed and chuckled at the same time.

"I know." Was she trying to make him feel even guiltier for staying away so long? His job as a teacher at a home for troubled teens in Vermont kept him busy during the school year, but this was the first summer he'd be spending back in Orchard Grove. "I know," he repeated and glanced around the room. Had they changed a single piece of furniture in the past decade?

"It's going to mean so much to Grandma Lucy to find out you've come all this way just for her." Her mom blew her nose loudly and stifled down another cry.

"Aw, come on." He chuckled. "You don't have to get like that." He wrapped his arm around her again. Had he gotten taller or was she shrinking?

She blew her nose one more time. "You have no idea how thankful I am to have you home." She reached up and patted his cheek as if he'd been seven years old. Some things would never change.

Like the bells that jingled on the front door when you walked in. Or the fact that this Safe Anchorage farm house was still standing, crooked staircase and all.

Or that his father was at this moment sitting in the den reading his newspaper or fishing magazine and wouldn't even make the time to greet his son who'd been away all these years.

Mom kept rubbing his back with one hand and wiping her cheeks with the other. He knew she'd get like this when he came home, but he wasn't prepared for how strongly her reaction would impact him.

This was his mother, the one who'd cleaned his skinned knees, taught him how to milk goats, taken out his multiple sets of stitches and kissed all his childhood scrapes and injuries away. When had she turned into an old woman?

He took a few steps down the hall, not in the direction of his father's den but toward the greenhouse Grandma Lucy had converted into her personal prayer retreat. He stopped and stared through the screen door into the dark room.

"Where's Grandma?"

"She's resting, honey." Mom frowned, the tears streaking down the wrinkles on her cheeks. "Grandma Lucy, like I told you, she's, well, she gets tired more easily now. She takes lots of naps these days."

"Yeah, I just thought she'd be in here." Brad cocked his head to the side. Had he ever seen Grandma Lucy's famous prayer chair empty in the middle of the afternoon?

"She's more comfortable in her room," Mom explained. "I told you we have her sleeping downstairs now, right? It's hard for her to manage the steps with her walker. You don't mind taking the attic space, do you?"

"Of course not." Hadn't he grown up in that room anyway? It was only once he became an adult that his mom thought he'd need the formal guest room for his infrequent visits.

She hugged him one last time. "Well, you get up and get your things settled. We've had lots of guests staying up there lately. Your cousin Jillian, I told you she was here earlier, didn't I?"

He nodded. Hard as it was for him to keep track of every single one of his dozens of cousins, he always listened more closely when Mom told him about how Jillian was doing. The two of them practically grew up together here in this very house — Brad, Jillian, and Jillian's brother. It was so long since any of them had been together.

Maybe he should have come sooner.

"So you showed up, hey, boy?"

The gruff voice knotted up Brad's stomach, and he turned. "Hey, Dad."

Mom clasped her hands together. "Hasn't he grown taller, Dennis?" she asked, her eyes darting nervously back and forth between both men.

Brad's father gave a grunt and tossed an old newspaper onto the dining room table. "Hope you're planning to help around the barn if you're gonna be staying here."

Mom nodded and prodded Brad toward the stairs. "Of course, of course. Now, you're tired after that long flight, so you go rest up, and I'll call you down when dinner's ready."

Brushing past his dad, Brad made his way to the stairs, skipping the one in the center that always squeaked, and shut himself into his tiny room in the attic.

He tossed his suitcase onto his bed and let out a mirthless chuckle.

No place like home?

We'll see about that.

CHAPTER 4

"Hi, Kitty." Megan tried to enunciate each word but hoped she wasn't dummying down her language too much. "I'm Megan." She thought back to when she first moved to Costa Rica. Had she felt as out of place then as she did now?

She gave Kitty what she hoped was a warm smile.

Blink.

Megan glanced at Scott. What did *blink* mean?

Susannah was massaging her sister's legs and glanced up. "Kitty, don't you think Scott and Megan look an awful lot alike? And you know what else? He's a year and a half older than she is, just like I'm a year and a half older than you."

Megan wondered how long it would take before she could talk to Kitty that comfortably. Granted, Susannah had quite a bit of a head start in experience and practice. Megan watched her as she kneaded Kitty's thigh muscles. Her legs were as skinny as Susannah's arms.

Forcing herself to stop staring, she stepped up to Kitty's

bed. "So have you ever heard of Costa Rica? That's where I live."

Blink.

Megan glanced at her brother again. She could be an old woman after spending her entire lifetime sharing the gospel completely independent of anybody else, but the minute her brother came into the room, she'd look to him to take the lead in a conversation.

Scott walked over to a world map taped above Kitty's dresser. "Right here," he said, pointing to the small country. "Costa Rica. We've talked about it before. Remember the story I told you about that naughty little monkey who stole my sunglasses when I was there visiting?"

Kitty let out a snort, and at first Megan was worried she was choking, but Scott laughed, and she realized Kitty was doing the same.

A girl with a sense of humor. Now Megan was starting to feel more comfortable. "Oh, that wasn't the worst," she added, chuckling herself at the memory. "After Scott got his sunglasses back, the monkey was so mad it started throwing mangoes at him. Do you know what mangoes are? It's a kind of fruit we have in Costa Rica. It kind of tastes like …"

She stopped herself. Was it rude to talk about food with someone who survived entirely on formula?

Susannah glanced up from her massage. Had Megan made some kind of irreparable mistake?

Scott sat on the corner of Kitty's bed, looking as comfortable as if he were reclining in a sauna. He was always so encouraging, which is why she'd turned to him that first Christmas in Costa Rica. He grinned at Kitty. "So tell me, kiddo, you still coughing up a bunch of green yucky guck today?"

Megan looked to Susannah, expecting her to answer for her sister, but she kept on massaging her legs and didn't respond.

Scott reached over and felt Kitty's forehead. "You've got to get better so the doctor doesn't have to come over here and put any of those nasty IVs in your arm. Did you eat your lunch today?"

Blink.

Scott sighed. "Well, you've got to promise to try a little harder at dinner, all right? You can do that for me, can't you?"

Blink. Blink.

He patted her shoulder. "That's my girl." He stood up and smiled down at Megan. "You want me to show you to your room?"

She nodded. Silly how she had traveled the world, spent

years as a missionary ministering to orphans living in some of the most heart-wrenching conditions, and her biggest worry was that Scott's new family might not like her.

"Come on." Scott looked back and smiled at her. He was nearly a foot taller than she was, but she remembered back to when they were little. Did he ever tell his wife about the way he'd dress up in their mother's skirts and jewelry to play house or castle with his baby sister?

The problem was no amount of make-believe could shield them from the unhappiness of their childhood.

She paused in the hallway, studying a framed wedding picture. Scott was holding Susannah in his arms, her long train draped over his shoulder and blowing in the breeze.

He looked so happy. So proud.

Like maybe he'd finally managed to forget everything he and Megan had gone through when they were young.

Whatever his secret was, she hoped he'd think to share.

CHAPTER 5

Brad had just finished unpacking his carry-on when his mother knocked on the door to his bedroom. It had been over ten years since he left home for good, but she still opened the door and let herself in.

"You resting?" she asked.

"Not anymore."

She sat on the edge of his bed. "Your father's reading his magazine."

Did she think he cared? "That's nice."

She gazed at him imploringly. He knew exactly what that look meant.

"Listen, Mom. I'm here for you, and I'm here for Grandma Lucy. But seriously, if Dad wants to talk to me, he knows how to walk up these old stairs just as well as you do."

Mom nodded. "I know. I know. I just wish ..." She let her voice trail off. How many times had they rehashed this exact same conversation? In the end, it didn't matter what she wished. Some people would never change, and there wasn't anything more to say about that.

"How's Grandma Lucy?" he asked, eager to change the subject. Even though she was technically his great-aunt, he had called her Grandma Lucy from the time he learned to speak. "Is she still asleep?"

Mom nodded. "I know we've already talked about it, but I want you to be prepared. She really hasn't been herself. I don't know what it is …"

"It's old age," he answered for her. "Simple as that."

She frowned and stared out the window. "I don't know …"

Forcing a smile, she rose to her feet. "Well, we're about to have dinner. I made stroganoff in the pressure cooker. Makes the meat more tender so it's easier for Grandma Lucy to chew. She's going to be so happy to see you home. I just know it."

Mom stared wistfully out the window then turned to him with a forced smile. "Well, come on now. You probably haven't had a proper home-cooked meal in ages."

Brad had told Mom a dozen times that he ate his meals with his students at the boys' home every night, but she still worried he must be starving. That was why she sent him care packages with homemade cookies and peanut brittle and other treats at least twice a month.

Most of the time, he figured his students looked forward to mail from Orchard Grove even more than he did.

He stood up, nearly bumping his head on the vaulted ceiling. It would take some getting used to, adjusting back to life at Safe Anchorage, but he was here for Grandma Lucy, and that made all the minor inconveniences worth it. In spite of his mom's many ominous warnings, he knew her condition couldn't be nearly that bad. Grandma Lucy was the strongest woman he knew — in just about every sense of the word.

"Connie!" Brad's father bellowed from the bottom of the staircase. "I thought you said it was time to eat. If that boy's gonna stay here, he's gonna eat when we tell him it's time to eat."

Mom gave Brad an apologetic glance and hurried to the staircase. "We're on our way, honey. We'll be right down."

She glanced back with the same hopeful expression in her eyes that some of Brad's students gave him when they handed in math tests they already knew they failed.

"Ready for dinner?"

Brad knew his mom well enough to understand what she was really asking him. If Brad's only plan was to pick a fight with his dad, he wouldn't have flown all the way from

Vermont to spend his summer break here in Orchard Grove.

He gave her a reassuring smile.

"Come on." He took his mom's arm in his. "Let's go down for dinner."

CHAPTER 6

The moment Brad saw Grandma Lucy sitting at the table in her wheelchair, he hated himself for staying away for so long. No matter how busy he got with the boys' home and his ministry in Vermont, no matter how much he hated the thought of spending a single day under the same roof as his father, he should have come home sooner.

Mom had told him Grandma Lucy lost some weight after her hospital stay last spring, but he had no idea she'd look like this. Like a ghost version of herself. A mere shadow.

He took her hand in his, almost surprised to find that there was still warmth left in it.

He leaned down and kissed her cheek. "Hi, Grandma Lucy. It's good to see you."

Her hand trembled when she brought it up to his face. Caressing his cheek, she began to pray in a warbling voice, "Father God, how I praise you for the grace you've shown us."

She brought down her hand. Was that all? In all the years

he'd known her, had she ever uttered a prayer that short?

Dad let out a grunt. "So we gonna eat, or we just gonna sit here and watch the food get cold?"

Mom was struggling to tie her checkered apron until Brad did it for her. While her back was turned to him, she let out another sniff, but he wasn't sure if she was getting emotional or just congested.

He took his spot next to Grandma Lucy in her wheelchair. Mom had told him she almost always needed help eating now. Keeping up with the farm animals, running the gift shop, and overseeing the production of all the Safe Anchorage goat soaps and lotions was enough to keep a woman half Mom's age perpetually busy. Not that his dad could be expected to lift a finger to help her. After a minor back injury put an end to his trucking days, Dad had been living here doing nothing but warming the couch and reading his stupid newspapers. If he realized how much Mom was working to take care of Grandma Lucy plus the goats plus the gift shop …

"Son, can you pass your father the rolls while they're still warm?" Mom asked.

Brad handed off the basket without making eye contact. If he was lucky, his dad would read his magazine all through dinner, and Brad could pretend he wasn't there. He was getting the feeling that taking care of Grandma Lucy alone was going to turn into his full-time summer job.

That's what happens when you get down on your knees and tell God you'll go anywhere he wants you to go.

When Brad first prayed that prayer last spring, he was thinking God might send him on another short-term mission trip to Mexico or somewhere else where he could use his Spanish language skills like he had every other summer.

Instead, the Almighty had brought him back here to the home of his childhood. It could be wonderful if it weren't for one thing.

"Tell your mother these are cold." Dad shoved the basket of biscuits in Brad's face.

Mom bustled from the stove where she'd been serving up the plates, but Brad scooted back his chair.

"I'll get it, Mom." He shot a glare at his dad, who was too absorbed in his fishing magazine to notice, yanked a paper towel from the dispenser, and shoved one of the bread rolls into the microwave. Nuke it for a full minute and then see if he thought it was too cold.

"Careful with that," his mother exclaimed, and Brad turned as Grandma Lucy spilled a cup of ice water down the front of her blouse.

"Great," Dad grumbled, shaking out his magazine as if it

could have gotten wet from the opposite end of the table. "Just great."

"Grandma Lucy, you all right?" His mother was bending down, trying to dry Grandma Lucy with one of those frilly doilies she kept on the table.

Brad yanked down a towel from above the sink. "I'll help, Mom." He knelt down by Grandma Lucy and started wiping her blouse.

"I dropped it," she said. "I made a mess."

He had never heard Grandma Lucy, who had always been so full of life and boldness and faith, sound so childlike.

"It's okay," he assured her, realizing he might be talking to himself as much as to her. He reached out for another rag Mom held out for him. "It's okay," he repeated.

Dad scooted back his chair noisily. "I'll eat my food in the den. Tell the boy to find a way to make himself useful and bring it in there."

CHAPTER 7

"This is some delicious bean soup." Megan wiped her mouth with her napkin and smiled at her sister-in-law.

"Well, it's not much," Susannah answered, "but I figured you'd be hungry after that long flight."

Scott nudged Megan in the side and grinned at his wife. "You know, babe, it was awful nice of you to make beans tonight because Megan was telling me on the drive over from the airport how they never seem to serve enough of those in Central America."

Susannah frowned. "Really? That's surprising."

Kitty sneezed, and while Susannah was busy wiping her face with a napkin, Megan gave her brother an annoyed glare.

Halfway into the meal, Scott got up and stood behind his wife's chair. "You've done enough now. I'll help Kitty finish the rest of dinner."

"No, I've got it," Susannah insisted, bringing the bottle of formula back to her sister's lips.

Scott leaned down and whispered, "Move over, babe. I've got it."

Susannah sighed loudly as her husband helped her to her feet.

It had been a good afternoon. Once Megan showered and changed out of her travel clothes, everyone had piled into Kitty's room to listen to *Adventures in Odyssey,* Kitty's favorite radio show. Susannah sat on Kitty's bed, cuddling and massaging her the whole time. Silly as it was, Megan had choked up, wondering what it might be like to grow up in a family this close to each other. At one point, she met her brother's eye and was almost certain he was thinking the same thing.

As it turned out, Kitty had a fabulous sense of humor. The fact that she happened to have cerebral palsy didn't change the way she enjoyed listening to the *Odyssey* stories, laughed at every silly joke, or loved her family.

A family that had opened their doors to Megan for the summer.

She had been so afraid of coming back to the States on furlough, which was why she had postponed the trip for several years. Up until recently, Scott was traveling the world with his mission work, and it wasn't like there was any other family worth visiting back in the States. Megan and Scott were each other's family, and now by extension so were Susannah and Kitty.

After switching their seats, Scott helped Kitty with her formula, and Susannah was finally able to eat more than a bite every two minutes. Megan tried to think of some way to fill the empty silence.

"So how are you feeling? Do you have much morning sickness?"

Susannah beamed at her. Megan had already noticed the way she practically glowed when talking about the pregnancy. "Oh, it's not been too bad." She patted her stomach. "And I know when he or she comes out it'll all be worth it."

"Don't listen to her," Scott mumbled. "She was upchucking five times a day until just a few weeks ago."

Kitty snorted on a laugh while Susannah exclaimed, "It wasn't that bad." How did she always look so peaceful and demure?

Megan couldn't picture anyone else more fit for motherhood or more perfect for her brother. "I still feel bad I missed your wedding. You know we're going to have to watch that video after dinner."

From her wheelchair, Kitty let out a massive snort, spraying milk out of her nose. What had Megan said wrong?

She turned to her brother, hoping he'd make the necessary apologies on her behalf, but he just wiped Kitty down and said, "Oh, you just want Megan to see how pretty you looked in your maid of honor dress, don't you? Didn't we talk about what the Bible teaches about vanity?"

Kitty made the same sound. Megan had to remind herself it was a laugh and not something to worry about.

While Scott cleaned up the sprayed milk, Susannah let out a surprised-sounding, "Oh," and jumped up from the table.

"Are you all right?" Megan blurted.

Scott hardly glanced at his wife. "Bathroom?" he asked with a grin.

Susannah nodded. "Sorry. Gotta run." She darted off down the hall. Kitty snorted again, and Scott closed the lid of her formula bottle. "All right. I think that's enough for today. What do you think?"

Blink, blink.

Scott nodded. "I think so too." He turned to Megan. "Not to get all mushy or anything, but have I told you how glad I am you're here?"

His smile sent a pang through her heart. During their childhood, how much healing might it have brought them both to see into the future and get a glimpse of Scott here with his family, so loving, so adored?

She shoved the thought quickly aside and returned his grin. "I'm glad I'm here too. It's going to be a great summer."

CHAPTER 8

"Brad, honey, will you please take this in to your father in the den? Tell him I found the June issue he's been looking for."

Brad stared at the fishing magazine and rolled his eyes.

"What?" Mom donned an innocent expression. "I'd take it myself, but I still have dishes to clean up."

"I told you I'd do them," he reminded her.

She shrugged. "If you want to help, be a good boy and take this in to your father, please."

Brad knew exactly what Mom was trying to do, and he didn't like it. How many times had he told her that he was coming for Grandma Lucy and nothing else? If Mom expected Brad's visit to turn into some cathartic reunion between father and son, he would have done better to stay at the boys' home in Vermont and save her the disappointment.

He glanced once more at his mother, whose arms were now covered in soapsuds up to the elbows, and grabbed the magazine from the kitchen counter. "Fine."

"Make sure you've taken your shoes off before you go into the den," she called out after him.

He ignored her remark and trudged down the hall in his shoes. This was why he would have preferred one of his summer mission trips like usual. Why had he come back to Orchard Grove at all? Grandma Lucy was already asleep. She didn't even need him here. Not right now, at least.

He stood outside the door of his father's den and knocked once. Without waiting for an answer he knew would never come, he stepped in.

"Mom told me to give this to you." He tossed the magazine onto his father's desk, rolling his eyes at this room that hadn't changed in decades. The only difference was a thicker layer of dust covering the books on the small shelf in the corner. As if his father might ever read anything besides a magazine or his beloved newspapers.

He glanced once more at his dad, who hadn't moved or made any indication he'd noticed Brad walk in, then turned around with a mumbled, "You're welcome."

"What'd you say, boy?"

Brad shook his head and didn't bother to face his dad. "Nothing. Just trying to help Mom tidy up the kitchen."

"Ask her if she's seen my June issue."

Brad turned around and pointed. "It's right there. Didn't

you hear me?"

Dad lowered his paper to glance at his desk. "Oh. Well, tell your mother to open a few windows before bed. It's stuffy as all get out in here."

Brad had to agree. "I'll let her know."

He paused at the door to glance back once at his father, but all he could see were two work-worn hands smudged with ink holding up that giant newspaper.

Brad shut the door behind him then went back into the kitchen to help Mom with the last of the dishes.

CHAPTER 9

Megan couldn't remember the last time she'd had her brother entirely to herself. Even when he flew out to comfort her during that first miserable Christmas in Costa Rica, there were dozens of kids running around and coworkers who needed her attention. Now it was just the two of them. Susannah and Kitty had gone to bed early, so Megan and Scott had the living room to themselves.

"You must be exhausted. I've kept you up way too late." Scott stretched his arms above his head. Even now that they were both adults, it was strange thinking of her brother getting tired.

Megan glanced at the clock in the living room. It was past midnight, but she felt like they'd need another five or six hours to catch up on the basics. She and Scott did their best to stay in touch, but a few quick emails or phone calls every so often certainly didn't make up for this face-to-face time.

It had been so long since they'd seen each other. He'd

changed some. Put on a little weight, probably thanks to eating all of Susannah's home-cooked meals. He looked older, which shouldn't have surprised her as much as it did. That was another thing about her brother. In her mind, he hadn't aged a day. He was still the same nineteen-year-old who cried when he said goodbye to her when he went off to Bible college.

Except now he had a wife who was expecting their first kid.

"I'm so glad you came," Scott said. "I think Susannah could use some female company."

Megan was about to point out that Susannah had her sister, but she stopped herself. As devoted as Susannah was to Kitty, it must be hard taking care of her day in and day out. What would it be like once the baby came?

"I just wish I could stay longer," she admitted. Susannah's due date was just two weeks after Megan was expected back at the orphanage.

Scott shook his head. "Don't worry about that. I know how busy you are in Costa Rica. How's the ministry down there, by the way?"

Had they really spent the past several hours without mentioning her work at all? She'd told her brother about a few of her coworkers and the children she worked with, but this was the first time he asked about the ministry in general.

"Things are going pretty well. We're up to seventy kids in the school and about thirty-five in the orphanage."

"Most of them young?"

She nodded. "Yeah, but we're adding some classes for teens and hoping to reach more people that way."

He smiled at her. "What about boys? You meet anybody else after that jerk from Vermont?"

She laughed. "Not exactly. There's not any time."

Thankfully, he didn't push the issue. "Well, I think it's great what you're doing."

She couldn't stop herself from rolling her eyes. "Too bad other people in the family don't see it that way."

There. The subject was broached.

Another one of those topics she was surprised it took them this long to get to.

Or maybe not so surprised after all.

Scott didn't respond right away, and for a minute Megan wondered if she'd made a mistake. Maybe she shouldn't have spoiled the mood like that.

"You talked to Mom lately?" His voice was far more subdued than it had been a minute earlier.

She shrugged. "Every so often. She'll email once or twice a month. Let me know how she's doing."

"And how is that?" he asked dryly.

She lowered her gaze, not wishing to meet his icy stare. "About the same."

"Dad still up to his same old tricks?" This time it was Scott who refused to make eye contact.

Another shrug. "Who knows?"

Scott let out a loud sigh, heavy with the painful memories they both shared.

"Yeah," he repeated without expression. "Who knows."

CHAPTER 10

Megan blinked at the clock in her brother's guest room. What was making that noise this early in the morning?

How long had she been asleep? Only a few hours?

Her back was aching after that bumpy bus ride and long flight yesterday. She grimaced as she sat up in bed and stretched.

Since she was awake, she might as well use the bathroom. And try to figure out where that sound was coming from. Could someone be running the vacuum cleaner at this hour of the night?

She padded down the hall and stopped in front of Kitty's open door. Susannah was leaning over her sister, sticking a tube down her throat.

"All better now?" Susannah turned off the small device by the bedside, and everything fell eerily quiet. She turned around. "Oh, I'm sorry. Did the suction machine wake you up?"

Megan shook her head. "No, I had to use the bathroom

anyway," she lied. She stepped into the room. "What is that?"

"It's Kitty's suction machine. We use it when she has a hard time swallowing."

Megan thought she remembered Scott mentioning something like that, but she hadn't been able to picture it until she actually saw it. "Is she okay?" Megan glanced at the bed. Had Kitty actually slept through that?

"Yeah," Susannah answered. "I heard her coughing in her sleep. There's a summer cold going around ..." Her voice trailed off. "Hey, I know you're probably exhausted, but I could use a cup of tea. Are you thirsty?"

Megan was about to decline, but Susannah looked at her so earnestly. What was it her brother had said about her being lonely for female friends?

Besides, now that Megan was awake, it would be hard to fall back to sleep.

"Sure," she answered. "Tea sounds nice."

A few minutes later, she and Susannah were nestled in a corner of the living room holding onto steaming mugs.

"This was my mom's favorite place to sit and read." Susannah smiled.

"Scott mentioned it wasn't that long ago that she died, was it?"

"Just a year," Susannah answered. Megan wondered if it would be better not to have said anything. She certainly didn't like to talk about her past. Was it different if you were someone like Susannah, who came from a strong, stable home? Or was it just as hard either way?

Maybe she should change the subject. She glanced down at her mug. Or maybe she should stop second-guessing everything and just ask Susannah directly.

She took in a deep breath and reminded herself that if her brother could fall in love with this woman, she was obviously someone Megan wanted to befriend. "Do you like to talk about your mom?" she asked. "Or does that just make it harder?"

Susannah's smile was soft and gentle. She rested her hand on her abdomen. "I like to talk about her. In fact, that's one of the hardest things now that she's gone. Scott never met her, and most everyone else acts like they've forgotten."

Megan was glad she hadn't made a terrible conversational blunder. "Tell me about her." She leaned forward in her seat and watched Susannah's smile broaden. "I'd love to hear more. What was she like?"

CHAPTER 11

Brad woke up a little before four in the morning. After spending a couple minutes in bed staring at the vaulted ceiling, he finally got out of bed. No use trying to go back to sleep when his body was still jetlagged and convinced it was time to rise. Besides, his mom would be getting up in just an hour or so, and she could use a hand with the goats.

In Vermont, he was used to starting his mornings with a run on the treadmill or the elliptical in the ministry center basement. Then he'd eat breakfast with the school staff before the kids arrived for classes. The evenings were meant to be his free time, but since he hated to cook, he usually ate dinner at the boys' home before retiring to his small studio apartment on the ministry headquarters campus.

There were no treadmills or ellipticals at his mom's, so he turned on the lights and threw on a pair of shorts to get ready for a run. At least he was up early enough to beat the Orchard Grove desert heat.

Slipping downstairs as quietly as he could, careful to

avoid the uneven step that squeaked in the center of the staircase, he headed to the kitchen and grabbed a cup of water. He was lacing up his running shoes when he heard a crash coming from the hall.

With his laces still untied, he hurried to investigate. The door was open to Grandma Lucy's prayer room.

"Grandma?"

He turned on the light and stepped into the room, nearly tripping over Grandma Lucy.

"What's wrong?" He knelt beside her. "Are you all right?"

"Went to the throne chair in the praying ..." she muttered.

"What happened?" he asked. "Did you fall? Are you hurt?" He ran his hands over her white hair, checking for any bumps or signs of injury.

"Princess in the rocking garden with my pillowcase still on."

"What are you saying?" He leaned down closer to her. Grandma Lucy was as tiny as Brad had been in fourth grade, but she was always so bold in spirit and speech. He could hardly believe that this mumbling, confused old woman was the Grandma Lucy he knew and loved.

"Are you hurt?" he asked again, hoping he might snap

her brain out of whatever fog it had fallen into. "Grandma Lucy," he repeated sternly. "Can you hear me? Can you tell me what happened?"

"They moved it this time."

"Moved what?"

The light in the hall flipped on, and Brad was staring at his father's slippers.

"She was trying to get to her prayer chair," Dad explained. "She wakes up in the middle of the night and wants to pray but forgets she can't walk." His voice was as gruff as ever, but for some reason Brad didn't detect the anger he'd grown to expect.

Dad squatted down and scooped Grandma Lucy up in his arms. She leaned her head against his shoulder. "Wanted my princess seat," she mumbled.

"I know you did, princess."

Brad couldn't remember ever hearing his father's voice sound that tender.

"Come on. Let's get you back to bed. Get you a little more sleep. You'll have plenty of time to talk to God in your prayer chair tomorrow."

CHAPTER 12

"I still can't believe you were intimidated by me," Megan exclaimed. She felt like she was a twelve-year-old again at a slumber party playing truth or dare. She and Susannah had been talking in the living room for over an hour.

Susannah's laugh was bright and musical. "And I can't believe you were intimidated either. Look at me." She gestured to her sweat-pants shorts and oversized T-shirt that probably belonged to her husband. "I mean, I'm not exactly a model anything right now."

Megan shook her head. "No, you're amazing. The way you take care of Kitty and are such a good wife, and even though you're pregnant, you've got the kindest, sweetest disposition. No wonder Scott could never stop raving about you any time we talked."

Susannah was beaming. "That's exactly how I feel about you. Ever since Scott and I started emailing each other, even before we met face to face, he was telling me all about this sister of his who loves God so much and goes around starting orphanages and teaching kids and ministering to others ..."

Megan shook her head. "It's not like that." At one point, she too had thought the life of a missionary was full of glory and glamour, but four and a half exhausting years on the field had stripped her of her unrealistic notions.

Susannah didn't seem convinced. "So how did you know God was calling you to the mission field?"

Megan wasn't sure if she was asking out of curiosity or if it had more to do with Susannah's past. When she and Scott first met, she had wanted to be a missionary but ended up in Orchard Grove to care for her sister after her mom's death.

"I definitely wasn't planning on serving internationally," she began. "After college, I heard about this girls' home in Vermont that needed counselors, and I liked the sound of it, so I moved out there. I loved the work, but I wasn't entirely convinced it was the right fit for me long-term. I'd been a Spanish major in school and didn't want to grow rusty, so I started looking into ministry opportunities in Latin America. That's when I heard about Kingdom Builders' work in Costa Rica."

"Was it hard for you to leave the States?" Susannah asked.

Megan shrugged. "Scott was already on the mission field, so he was traveling all over by then. And I'm sure he's told you some about our family."

Susannah stared at her lap.

"So in short, no, it wasn't that hard," Megan replied quietly. "I guess the most difficult part was leaving the girls' home. I'd only been working there for a year, but I loved the ministry there. It's really special when you get to live and eat and sleep and do everything together." She stared past Susannah's shoulder, trying to forget bittersweet memories from her time in Vermont. "It's probably the closest thing I'd felt to a family my whole life." She added quickly, "But I know God's called me to Costa Rica, so I'm glad to be there."

Phew. She'd gotten close to saying too much.

Susannah was staring at her empty mug. "I sometimes wonder what it would have been like if I'd gotten to go on the mission field."

She sounded so sad, Megan immediately tried to cheer her up. "You never know what's going to happen, right? I mean, you're still young, and Scott's been in missions even longer than I have. I'm sure God has something in store for you two."

Susannah nodded. "It's probably sinful of me, so I guess

I can make this a confession of sorts, but I've been a little jealous of you. I mean, not necessarily you personally, but people like you. Nothing tying you down, nothing keeping you from going wherever God leads ..." Her voice trailed off.

Megan had heard similar sentiments when she left the girls' home. At the time, she had smiled, listening while others praised the seemingly romantic life of a missionary, but she felt close enough to Susannah to be more truthful.

"Honestly, if there's anyone to be envied, it's you. I mean, being a missionary definitely has its rewards, but sometimes I tell God I'd just like to settle down and live with air conditioning and speak English all day and not have to eat beans at every meal ..." She stopped when she saw Susannah's face. "I mean, it's not that I dislike beans, and the ones you made for dinner were great, but it's just that ..." She gave up trying to backpedal and jumped straight to her apology. "I'm sorry. I shouldn't have said anything about that. But you know what I mean."

"There's no place like home, right?" Susannah offered with a warm smile.

Megan nodded. "Right. That's what I miss. The girls' home job was stressful, but at least it felt like home. It felt like family. In Costa Rica, it's just as stressful. Even more so because we have the language barrier and all kinds of political issues that come up, and there's never enough resources for us to help everyone in need, and sometimes the people we try to help won't accept it, so yeah. It's not all that glamorous when you look at it like that."

Susannah bit her lip and asked somewhat shyly, "What about boyfriends? Is there anyone in your life at all?"

Megan sighed. They'd talked about just about everything else. Why not this too? Scott knew all about Megan's past. There was no reason his wife shouldn't as well. "Well, I met someone back in Vermont, but he didn't start working there until I had already committed to the orphanage. We tried long-distance for a little bit, but it wasn't like you and Scott. It just didn't work out."

"I'm sorry."

She shrugged. "It's fine. It was years ago. I think if I had stayed in Vermont, it might have been different, but I definitely felt called to Costa Rica, and he definitely didn't, so there wasn't a whole lot we could do to change that or make it work out in the end. So don't feel bad. It was for the best."

Even as she said the words, Megan wondered if she sounded insincere.

Both women stopped talking when they heard the toilet

flush down the hall.

"So there you two are. I hope you're not telling each other too many embarrassing stories about me." Scott stood outside the bathroom grinning.

Susannah stood up and went to him. "Not at all. We were just catching up."

"Do you have any idea what time it is?" he asked.

She nodded. "We should probably try to get a little more sleep, don't you think?"

"Sounds like a good plan." Megan stood up with a sigh. "Thanks for the tea. I guess I'll see you in a little bit."

Megan watched as her brother wrapped his arm around his wife and led her back to their bedroom. For a minute, she was tempted to pour herself another mug of tea, but she figured it was probably cold by now anyway. Besides, after staying up late talking to Scott and then spending another hour or longer out here with Susannah, it really was time for her to get some rest.

If only she could slow her mind down enough to try.

CHAPTER 13

"You woke up that early?" Brad's mom asked with a frown. "You poor thing. You'll have to try to nap this afternoon."

"It's fine," he told her. "I'm still on East Coast time. It was like waking up any other day."

"Yeah, but you stayed up so late," she protested. Brad had to smile at the way his mother and just about everyone else in Orchard Grove considered a nine o'clock bedtime late.

They were out in the barn milking the goats. It was still early, but he could tell it was going to be another hot day. After his dad had put Grandma Lucy back to bed, Brad sat in her room with her to make sure she was all right, but she was fast asleep in a few minutes, so he'd taken himself on that run around Baxter Loop. Good thing too, since the temperature was already in the low eighties.

His mom led the goat they'd just milked back to her stall and brought another up to the stand. "This is Peaches. She's the one I told you about. See, her coat's pink."

He nodded. When his mom called him to talk about her pink goat, he hadn't believed her. Even the pictures made the animal appear more beige than anything else, but now that he saw Peaches in person he had to admit his mom was right.

Who'd ever heard of a pink goat?

He sat down on the milking stool, which was far too small for him, but at least it saved his mom from the work. With over a dozen goats in milk, it was too big a job for someone her age.

"Grandma Lucy fell this morning," he told her as he worked his hands into a good rhythm. If milking a goat was like riding a bike, his cramped thumb muscles certainly didn't think so.

Mom shook her head. "I know. Your father told me after he got her back to bed. She gets forgetful, you know. Doctor says it's dementia."

It didn't make sense. Grandma Lucy had practically half of the Bible memorized. Her mind was as sharp as ever. At least it had been until her most recent hospital stay last spring.

"I'm just glad we don't have to put her in the assisted living home. I'd hate to do that to her."

Brad didn't respond. He agreed with his mother in

principle. Who would actually want to live in a home for the frail and the elderly, removed from all comforts of home and separated from your family?

On the other hand, his mom was in no shape to be taking care of Grandma Lucy and all these goats and the Safe Anchorage gift shop full-time. If his dad would ever get out of his chair and put down that blasted newspaper, maybe the two of them together could manage, but Brad knew that was far too much to expect.

Or maybe that wasn't fair. He'd never seen his father act as tenderly as he had with Grandma Lucy. Maybe he was doing more than Brad knew.

Or maybe this morning was just a fluke.

Peaches snorted, and Mom scratched the animal between her ears. "You silly little girl. You know the sooner you let us milk you, the sooner you can go be with that sweet little baby of yours." She turned to Brad. "She's the one who had that little buckling who likes to climb the jungle gym you used to play on."

"You still have that plastic thing?" Brad asked. "Why do you hold onto it?"

Mom busied herself nuzzling Peaches' nose and holding out sunflower seeds for her to eat out of her hand. "We have kids come here all the time on field trips or with their families who stop at the gift shop. Besides, one day there might be grandkids around to play on it. Who knows? I certainly wouldn't mind becoming a grandmother."

Brad was so used to his mother hinting at his love life he didn't even bother getting annoyed but kept his focus on his milking. He could tell Peaches had recently kidded because her supply seemed never-ending.

"I don't see why you haven't settled down yet," Mom went on. "Aren't there lots of nice Christian gals working at that girls' home?"

He was glad to have the milking to focus on. "Being nice and being Christian aren't the only requirements, you know. I just haven't met the right one yet."

Mom frowned. "Well, maybe you're just being too picky. I hate to be the one to say it, but I'll go ahead and say it anyway. You haven't been the same since that girl you liked moved down to Haiti or wherever it was she went to become a missionary."

He rolled his eyes. He'd told Mom that story years ago and had regretted it ever since. "It just wasn't meant to be, Mom. Wasn't meant to be."

She let out a disappointed *harrumph.* "So it seems. But what I don't get is why you haven't given any other girl a second glance since then. And if the first one was all that good to start with, well, maybe you should have never let her get away in the first place."

He shook his head. Just like it was pointless hoping to ever have any sort of meaningful relationship with his dad, it was just as useless talking to his mom about his love life. Some things wouldn't change.

Peaches stamped her foot, and Mom grabbed the milk bucket out just in time to keep her from kicking it over. "Oh, you naughty thing," she exclaimed while giving the goat another handful of sunflower seeds.

Brad sighed, thankful to end this awkward conversation about a relationship that was obviously doomed from the start with a girl he was certain he'd never see again.

CHAPTER 14

Megan stumbled out of the guest room after just a few hours of sleep, still wearing her pajamas and groggy from staying up so late talking. Scott and Susannah were at the couch, and Megan froze in the hallway when she saw her brother's face. "What's wrong?"

Scott frowned and rubbed Susannah's shoulder.

"It's Kitty," he explained without looking up. "She's got another fever."

"Uh-oh." Megan stepped into the living room. "Is there anything I can do to help? Does she need something?"

Scott shook his head. "We're friends with her doctor. She's on her way over now."

Megan was about to joke about how she'd better change out of her pajamas, but the mood in the room was so heavy she stopped herself and instead took the seat next to Susannah.

"Are you two okay?" she asked quietly.

Susannah nodded, and Scott answered for her. "It's just

hard. We thought she'd gotten over her pneumonia last month, but there's been this summer cold going around, and Kitty's had a lingering cough, and she's gotten to the point where the antibiotics don't always work as efficiently as we'd like them to."

Megan didn't know what to say. She frowned at her brother sympathetically. "Is she awake? Does she need some company or anything?" She tried to force a smile. "Didn't that last *Adventures in Odyssey* end on a cliffhanger?"

Any attempt to lighten the mood failed. Megan stared at the table.

There was a knock on the door, and Scott patted his wife's back. "Stay here, babe. I'll let Janice in."

Megan wished she could turn herself into the touchy-feely type. Susannah looked like she could use a shoulder to cry on or at the very least a strong hug, but Megan worried that anything she tried to say or do would sound forced and trite. What did she know about having a sister with cerebral palsy? What did she know about the worry that comes when a loved one falls ill? She imagined all Susannah had gone through in the past year — losing her mother, becoming her sister's sole caregiver, marrying Scott, getting pregnant. How did she handle all those changes and still maintain such a sweet temperament?

"Thanks for coming," Scott was saying. "Megan, this is Janice."

Megan turned around to look at the doctor. She was younger than she had expected, with long hair and a complexion like a model's.

Susannah stood up and led the doctor into Kitty's room.

"What's her fever at?" Janice asked.

"It was 103.2 when I last checked."

Megan stayed in the living room, figuring they didn't need another body in Kitty's small room, getting in the way and offering no real help. Since she couldn't do anything tangible for Kitty at the moment, she bowed her head and tried to pray, but all she could think about were the kids back in Costa Rica. She'd felt so ready for this vacation. She wasn't expecting to miss them this much.

Maybe that was the missionary's curse. When you were on the field, you longed for the familiarity of home. Then once you got there, you were homesick for the land and the people you'd left behind.

She let out her breath, trying to clear her mind so she could pray for Kitty.

For right now at least, it was all she could think to do.

CHAPTER 15

Mom pulled the cinnamon rolls out of the oven then hurried to pour Dad's cup of coffee.

"I wish you'd let me help." Brad hated watching her work herself so hard the moment she came in from milking all those goats.

"Don't worry about me," she called out with a tired-sounding chuckle in her voice as she set Dad's cream and sugar in front of him. "But if you want to be a dear, you can go tell Grandma Lucy it's time for breakfast and see if she wants help into her wheelchair or if she feels up to using the walker."

"Woman's too clumsy to be using that walker," Dad grumbled without looking up from his magazine.

Brad didn't respond and made his way to the bedroom. When he saw her on the floor, he rushed into the room. "Grandma? Are you all right? Did you fall again?"

He knelt beside her. Once he was closer, he could hear her talking to herself. At least she was more coherent than she'd been last night.

"May you keep him covered in your peace and in your love, may he rest in the assurance that you are the God of his life, the sovereign over creation, the king of the universe. Show him your power ..."

She stopped with her mouth open when she noticed Brad beside her and blinked a few times. "You're here."

"Yeah, Grandma. I came last night. Don't you remember?"

"Last night?" she repeated. "Where was I?"

"You were sleeping, but then we had dinner together. Do you remember that?"

Grandma Lucy let out a chuckle. "Well now, would you look at that? I ended up on the floor again. How do you think I got there, do you suppose?"

"You must have fallen. Are you hurt?"

She shook her head. "I don't think so. Do I look hurt?"

"You look lovely," he told her.

She swatted at him playfully. "Now, you cut that out. Did you say it's time for dinner?"

"No. But Mom made cinnamon rolls."

She blinked at him. "Mom's here?"

"My mom. I'm talking about Connie. Your niece."

"What about her now?

"She made cinnamon rolls."

"Connie did? I hope she didn't burn herself."

"I'm sure she's fine." He helped her to her feet. "Are you hungry? Want to get in your wheelchair, and we'll go eat?"

"Have you called Floyd in?"

Brad's hands clammed up. "Who?"

"Floyd. Does he know it's lunch? He's been working hard in the barn, hasn't he?"

"Grandpa Floyd's not here."

"Oh. He's not?"

"No." Brad swallowed, wondering what he was supposed to say about the grandfather who'd been dead for decades.

"I thought I heard him out there."

"Maybe that was Dennis you heard."

Grandma Lucy studied him as he wheeled the chair closer to her. "Dennis? No, you're Dennis, aren't you?"

He swallowed. "No, I'm Brad. Dennis's son."

She nodded. "Oh, that's right. I was just praying for you. Did I tell you that?"

"That's wonderful, Grandma. Thanks so much." If he'd known Grandma Lucy's dementia was this bad, he would have come home years ago.

He helped her into her chair, and she held her hand in

his. Her skin was so soft for someone her age. "Now, what'd you say your name was?"

"I'm Brad."

She smiled. "Brad. That's right. Are you a Christian, Brad? Have you been born again?"

"Yes, Grandma. I work at a home for teen boys, remember? I'm sort of like a missionary there."

"A missionary?"

"Yeah. A missionary."

"You've got to have a lot of prayers to be a missionary, don't you?"

"Sure do."

"Well, once we're done giving me my checkup, I'll tell you what. I want to pray for you every day when you're on the mission field, so why don't you just tell me your name, and I'll write it down in my journal so I don't forget. Sound like a good plan?"

Brad swallowed painfully. "Sure thing. That sounds like a really good idea."

CHAPTER 16

It was official. Megan was too worried about Kitty to offer up anything but short, distracted prayers. She got up from the table and made her way down the hall, where the doctor was talking to Scott and Susannah.

"I don't think it will do any good to take her to the hospital just yet. We want her to get as much rest as she can, and it's going to be important to push fluids as much as possible. If we're lucky, we can avoid the IV."

Susannah let out a heavy sigh. "Thanks, Janice. I really appreciate you coming over here like this."

The doctor smiled. "I just wish I had a magic wand that would make her feel better. I know you do too."

Scott started walking toward the front door, and Megan had to step aside to let everybody pass.

"Thanks again for coming by," he told the doctor.

She paused with her hand on the doorknob. "I'm on call tonight, but otherwise I've got the weekend off. Just let me know if anything changes, and we'll be in touch."

Susannah reached out to give the doctor a hug, and Janice put her hand on Susannah's belly. "And don't forget to ask for help when you need it. You need to be taking care of yourself too."

Susannah smiled, and Megan wondered if pregnancy automatically made you comfortable with having your belly rubbed like that without invitation.

Janice let herself out the door, and Scott shut it gently behind her. Wrapping his arm around his wife, he gave her a kiss on the top of her head. "You doing okay, babe?"

She rested her cheek against his chest. Now that they were standing next to one another, Megan realized how much taller her brother was. "I'm okay. I'm glad she stopped by."

Scott smiled. "One of the perks of being related to the town's only pediatrician, right?"

So that explained the familiarity of a home visit and the departing pat on the belly.

"So what did the doctor have to say?" Megan asked, uncertain how much she had missed while everyone was in Kitty's room.

Scott and Susannah looked at each other as if silently deciding who would answer.

"Her lungs don't sound as clear as the doctor would

like," Scott explained, "but with rest and prayer and a lot of fluids, it might end up just fine. It's one of those times where we'll just have to wait and see."

"That's the hardest part," Susannah admitted, still leaning against Scott's chest.

"Is she asleep?" Megan asked.

Susannah nodded. "She hardly ever sleeps this long in the morning. That's one reason why I started to get worried."

Megan knew plenty of coworkers from Costa Rica who would know exactly what to say to give Scott and Susannah the encouragement they obviously needed, but all Megan could offer was a lame, "Well, I hope she gets better soon."

Scott nodded. "Me too. Come on. Let's see what we can pull together for lunch." He turned and gave Megan a wink. "If we dig around a little bit, I bet we can find some more beans."

CHAPTER 17

"Why didn't you tell me the dementia was this bad?"

Brad knew it was unfair to get upset with his mom like this, but he had no idea who else to blame.

Mom stood hunched over a sink full of soapy water. "It's not like it's been happening for that long, honey. It came on all of a sudden after her heart attack."

He shook his head. "Things like this don't happen all of a sudden. There are warning signs. You don't go from being fully alert like she's always been to someone who can't even remember her husband's dead." His throat clenched up, but he managed to get out the words.

"I'm certain of it," Mom repeated. "This is all new."

"Well, you need to talk to the doctor."

"I have." The rising intensity in her voice matched his own. What was the worst was that he knew how foolish it was to be mad at his mom, but he didn't feel like he had any other choice. She should have told him. He would have come months ago, whether or not he was needed at the boys' home.

He got up from his chair. This wasn't a conversation he could handle sitting down. "What'd the doctor say?"

"He said it's dementia, plain and simple. Gave her some tests, said it was inconclusive but it's a good indication she's going to get Alzheimer's."

"She's not going to get Alzheimer's," he shot back. "She already has it."

Mom wiped her hands on a dishtowel and turned to face him. "Now listen, honey. I know she gets confused sometimes, but that's ..."

"She didn't know who I was." How could he make his mother understand? Grandma Lucy, who'd been in every single major memory of his childhood, didn't know who he was.

"It couldn't have been all that bad. It must have been a mistake." Mom's voice was quiet. Uncertain.

"She didn't know who I was," Brad repeated firmly.

Mom sniffed. Great. Now she was going to start crying, and Brad would be left feeling like the villain. It wasn't fair. Mom saw Grandma Lucy every day. That's probably why she hadn't realized just how bad things were. The change must have been gradual. A heart attack couldn't make someone's brain deteriorate like that overnight. Mom was just too close to Grandma Lucy and couldn't see. Either that or she was in complete denial.

Mom straightened her checkered apron. "Now, I know she wakes up confused sometimes, and she tries to get to her prayer room without her walker, but she's still our Grandma Lucy. She's still there."

He shook his head. She didn't understand, and he had to make her. "She looked right at me and asked if I'd seen Floyd."

Mom bit her lip. Maybe now it was starting to sink in.

"She asked me where Floyd was, and then she looked right at me and wanted to know if I'd been born again. Just like she asks the first time she meets anyone. She didn't know who I was."

"That's because you've been gone so long," came a low grumble.

Brad whipped his head around at the unwelcome sound. Since when was his dad in the habit of coming out of his den for anything other than meals?

Mom fidgeted with her hair. "Now, Dennis, don't you get worried. Let me pour you some coffee, and we'll try to keep our voices lower so we don't bother you."

"Bother me?" Dad took a step forward. "Why should I be bothered? Just because some son of mine comes wandering home after God only knows how long and blames us for the way we're looking out for Grandma Lucy? You want to get upset with your mama, boy? You want to tell her how bad things have gotten with Grandma Lucy? Do you? Is that why you came here, just to get your mama upset?"

Mom wiped her teary cheeks and forced a smile. "Now, Dennis, why don't you let me finish these dishes, and I'll send Brad over to the gift shop to see if they need any more cinnamon rolls over there. Then you can go back and ..."

"I don't care about the gift shop, woman." Dad pounded the dining room table. Mom jumped, but Brad clenched both his teeth and his fists while Dad continued hollering. "That boy should have been taught a lesson in respect a good long while ago, and until he can treat you proper-like, he's got no business here."

Mom hurried to position herself between Brad and his father. She was so short Brad could still stare straight at his dad.

"Now, Dennis," she began.

"Don't you *now Dennis* me, woman. You're the one who begged this boy to come home, and I'm the one who told you there'd be nothing but trouble if he did." He let out a rude scoff. "Mr. High and Mighty, coming back home after his grand adventures saving the world for Jesus Christ, but he can't be here a full day without disrupting the peace and making you feel bad. Look at her, boy." Dad pointed his finger in mom's face. "You think a real man would make his mama cry like this?"

Mom sniffed loudly and hurried out of the room. Brad was about to follow after her, but dad took a step to the side, blocking his way.

"You let her be. And I swear that if you cause one more ounce of trouble in this house ..." He left the thought unfinished, probably because he couldn't think of any threat he could actually carry out.

Brad had promised himself, God, and his mother that he'd avoid trouble for the time he was here in Orchard Grove. He hadn't traveled all the way to Washington to pick a fight with his dad, not after all these years. It wasn't even water under the bridge anymore. It was a riverbed as dried up as the one that ran through the center of town, and that was all.

Brad took a step forward, but his dad grabbed him by the arm. "Where you think you're going?" he snarled.

Brad shoved his dad's hand away, stomped to the back door, and threw on his running shoes. If he didn't want to do something he'd have to repent of later, it would be wise to get as far away from his father as was humanly possible in a town this small.

Ignoring the midday heat, he stormed off the porch, slamming the door behind him and took off running.

CHAPTER 18

"Are you sure you don't mind staying here with Kitty all by yourself?" Susannah asked for what must have been the tenth time or more.

Scott was practically pushing her out the front door. "Yes, I'm sure. You need the fresh air and something to get your mind off everything here."

"What about work?" she asked.

"That's why it's called the weekend," Scott reminded her, then turned to Megan. "You make sure to keep her out for as long as you can, all right? And you both have your cell phones so I can be in touch if anything changes with Kitty. Now go. Have fun. Do girly stuff, treat yourselves to some ice cream, I don't care what you do. Just leave me alone so I can have a little peace and quiet while I watch the Red Sox."

Susannah gave him a playful push. "Don't give me that. You know you're going to be buried in your missionary books until we get back."

He shrugged. "Probably. But I'll at least pretend like I'm

71

taking the weekend off. Just like you two should."

He gave Susannah one last hug, then she and Megan walked toward the car in the driveway. Megan was glad the two of them had spent last night gabbing. Any discomfort she initially felt with her sister-in-law had disappeared, which would certainly make their day out together less awkward.

"So where do you want to go?" Susannah asked. "There's a little ice cream place not too far, or some nice trails by the riverbed if you want to go on a walk, or there's a farmer's market in front of the courtyard."

Megan really didn't care where they went, but she didn't want to be the kind of guest who refused to make up her mind. "How about the farmer's market? That sounds fun."

Susannah smiled as she pulled out of the driveway. "You want to know something? I was hoping you'd say that."

The car's air conditioning was broken, so they drove with the windows down. It was hot, but Megan was thankful for the fresh air. It was nice to ride on a smooth, paved road for a change too.

Susannah was quiet. Was she worried about her sister? And would it make matters worse if Megan asked about Kitty? Were they just supposed to pretend they were out to spend a carefree day around town?

"So what do you think so far of Orchard Grove?"

Megan was grateful Susannah was the one to break the silence.

"It seems like a nice little place to live. I bet you're excited to be raising your family here."

Susannah didn't respond right away, and Megan turned the question around. "What about you? What do you think of Orchard Grove?"

Susannah paused before answering. "I guess there are advantages and disadvantages to living somewhere where just about everybody knows everybody else. But then something funny happens, and you meet someone who's been here for years, and you wonder how you could have gone that whole time without knowing each other. That's how it was with my mom and stepdad at least."

"Yeah, Scott told me a little bit about their story. They'd only been married for a few months, hadn't they?"

Way to go, Megan, she thought to herself. She was supposed to be coming up with ways to get Susannah's mind off her sick sister, not make her even more depressed.

"Derek's a great guy." At least Susannah was still smiling. "I'm sure you'll meet him soon. Janice, she's Kitty's doctor that you met back at the house, that's his sister."

"Oh. I was wondering what Scott meant when he said she was related."

"Yeah, she's technically my step-aunt, but she's closer to my age than Derek's, and he basically raised her from the time she was a little girl, so it's closer to having another sister. Or something like that."

"Yeah," Megan found herself replying. "Or something."

Susannah pulled in front of a little courtyard with tents and booths. "Here's where we have the farmer's market every Saturday. It's tiny, but it's actually fairly impressive for a town this size. Care to look around?"

She parked the car, and Megan got out. It was hot, but at least without the humidity she was used to in Costa Rica. Susannah came up beside her. "There's all the farmers here, obviously, but they have a lot of handmade crafts and things too. Maybe we can find a present to take back to Kitty to cheer her up. Come on. Let's take a look."

CHAPTER 19

Brad wasn't used to running so much, especially not in this type of desert heat. He made his way to the trail that ran alongside the dried-out riverbed through the center of town. The worst part wasn't his shin splints or the way the heat radiated up to his face when he ran along the black pavement. The worst part was knowing that he'd eventually have to turn around and head home and try to smooth things over with his dad. For his mother's sake if nothing else.

Forgive those who sin against you. Go the extra mile. Turn the other cheek. Brad had spent these past few weeks preparing for his trip back home, meditating on the sermon on the Mount, but even that hadn't stopped him from nearly blowing up at his dad this morning. At least compared to their epic battles in the past, today's confrontation was little more than a scrimmage.

As he neared the courtyard, he wondered why so many people had gathered. That's right. Today was Saturday. People would be here for the farmer's market. He thought about heading home, figuring anyone he ran into wouldn't appreciate standing around and reminiscing while he was drenched in sweat, but he still needed a little bit of time to calm down. Besides, the majority of people who lived in Orchard Grove were old enough to be his grandparents and were such busybody gossips he didn't care what they thought about his pit-stained T-shirt. If only he'd brought his wallet, he could get himself a snack or something refreshing to drink.

"Brad Gregory? Is that you?

He turned around to face Mrs. Porter, who had been his fourth-grade teacher as well as his high school principal. She stood staring at him with the pinched face that Brad guessed was her closest approximation to a smile.

"Hi, Mrs. Porter. It's good to see you."

She gave a curt nod. "You're here visiting Lucy, I assume? How is she?"

Brad was about to tell her how Grandma Lucy had forgotten who he was, but then he remembered who he was talking to. Mrs. Porter was the president of Orchard Grove Bible Church's Women's Missionary League and probably the biggest gossip the town had seen in a century. He forced a smile. "She's doing great. Gaining her strength back every day."

Mrs. Porter sniffed dubiously. "Really?" She cocked her head to the side, making her earrings jingle.

Brad smiled. "Yeah, just last night she made it down the hall without her walker or wheelchair or anything." His mom had drilled into his head when he was a child the importance of telling the truth, and he was impressed at the way he had managed to avoid any technical falsehoods.

Mrs. Porter raised her eyebrows in what appeared to be sincere surprise. "That's great news. Please tell her we're all praying for her."

"I will." Before Mrs. Porter could ask him anything else about his family or his personal life, Brad excused himself. He glanced around at the Main Street businesses, trying to guess which one would be most likely to have a drinking fountain inside.

A flash of black hair caught his attention.

His heart raced.

Maybe he needed a drink more than he realized. He spotted the bank and decided it was as good a place as any. Even if there wasn't a drinking fountain, he knew they had a bathroom there, or at least they'd had one years ago when he still lived here. Worst case scenario, he could splash some water on his face at the sink.

He glanced once more at where he had seen the young

woman with the black hair, then made his way across the street. The heat must really be getting to him if he could be in the middle of Orchard Grove and think he saw Megan Phillips, a girl from so long ago in his past.

A girl he knew he'd never see again.

CHAPTER 20

Susannah looked across the street toward the bank. "What are you staring at over there?"

Megan hadn't realized she'd been so obvious. "Oh, nothing." She glanced back once more to convince herself that she hadn't really seen who she thought she had.

Susannah was still craning her neck. "Is there something interesting over there?"

Megan sighed. "No, I just thought I saw someone familiar for a minute. Someone I knew a long time ago."

"Really? What'd they look like? Maybe I know them."

She shook her head. "No, he doesn't live anywhere near here, and it was so long ago I doubt I'd recognize him anymore."

Susannah raised her eyebrows. "Is there a story behind this?"

Megan couldn't hide her smile. "Not really."

Susannah elbowed her playfully in the side. "Are you sure? Because you had a look in your eyes just like Scott gets before he says something really romantic."

Megan shrugged. "It's nothing. It's that guy I told you about last night, the one I met in Vermont."

"Did you ever date him?"

"Kind of. But I was already committed to Costa Rica. I just had a few months left to finish up my year at the girls' home, and we didn't see each other after that."

"You said you tried the long-distance thing, didn't you?" For a conversation they had at four in the morning, Susannah sure had a memory for detail.

"We tried," Megan answered, "but it didn't work out."

"No?"

Megan hadn't meant to get worked up, but she realized her heart was racing, and she forced herself to calm down. How long ago was it? There was no reason to get angry all over again.

"He was supposed to come out and visit, but then there was this big storm and we had to postpone. A week later, he sent me an email and said he'd changed his mind." She shrugged, as if trying to convince herself the story couldn't still bother her after so many years. "He said he felt called to work at the boys' home, and since I was called to Costa Rica, it was probably God's way of telling us it wouldn't work."

"I guess I could see that," Susannah answered. "At first

we thought God's call would keep Scott and me from ever being together too."

Megan straightened her hair, which was blowing in the summer breeze. "Yeah, well, found out he was dating one of my former coworkers from the girls' home. So I'm not really sure how much God's call had to do with it." She shrugged again. "But it's fine. It was just weird seeing someone who looked like him, that's all."

She'd been over him for years. It didn't make sense for him to pop into her mind now all of a sudden, unless it had something to do with being here in Orchard Grove with Scott and his new wife. They were so much in love and so perfect for one another, it was no wonder Megan was out here thinking about Brad Gregory.

About a man she'd never see again and may as well do her best to forget entirely.

CHAPTER 21

Megan couldn't have spent more than ten minutes so far at the farmer's market, but she could already understand what Susannah meant when she talked about everyone in Orchard Grove knowing everybody else. Megan had lost track of how many people stopped Susannah to ask about Kitty or the pregnancy.

"Good afternoon, Susannah," a pinch-nosed woman with gaudy rings on her fingers greeted. "Who are you here with today?"

Susannah stopped and smiled pleasantly. Megan wondered if the look was practiced or if her sister-in-law really was that kind. No wonder her brother fell in love with her.

"Hi, Mrs. Porter. This is Scott's sister, Megan."

The woman sniffed as she shook Megan's hand. "Are you a missionary too by any chance?"

Megan wasn't sure if Mrs. Porter had made a lucky guess or if she knew something about her already. "I am. I work in

Costa Rica."

Mrs. Porter raised her nose in the air and sniffed again. "My dear, what a dreadful earthquake that was. How long do you think it will take for all the rebuilding?"

"Well, the big earthquake was actually back in the '90s. I'd say most everything is up where it should be now."

"Dreadful," Mrs. Porter remarked. "Just dreadful. My husband and I, we're big supporters of Christian Relief Ministries. You know the organization I mean? The one that Cameron Hopewell's son runs. It's like the Red Cross, except it's Christ-centered. These big disasters strike, and everyone sends their money to the Red Cross, but you know it's not a Christian organization in spite of its name. In fact, would you believe that in Muslim countries they actually call themselves something else? Can you imagine a greater affront to God than that?" She snorted. "As if the cross is something to be ashamed of."

She turned her head to Susannah. "What's wrong, dear? You're positively pale."

Susannah grabbed Megan's arm. "Sorry, Mrs. Porter, but I need to run to the gas station and use the bathroom."

Mrs. Porter pinched her lips together even more tightly. "Pregnancy bladder, is it? I hear cranberry juice helps with that. And there are some exercises my daughter told me about. You can do them to keep yourself from leaking after the baby comes. You'll have to look it up on the web because I'm sure I couldn't explain it to you. Well, I can see you've got to run. But you don't want to go into that gas station, I assure you. Last time I was in there I saw a dead mouse in one of their traps. Can you believe it? It was dead, completely dead, just lying there. If you need the ladies' room, there's a nice one in the bank right across the street. It's nice to meet you, Maddie. We've all found it very interesting now that your brother's moved to Orchard Grove."

Megan didn't bother to ask what the old woman meant but followed her sister-in-law, who was nearly running to get to the bank across the street.

CHAPTER 22

"I thought she'd never stop talking. I'll just be a minute," Susannah panted as she raced into the women's room.

Megan stared around the bank and finally made herself comfortable in one of the oversized chairs by the door. At least the building was air conditioned. She'd left her phone in Susannah's car and didn't have anything to do other than wait. Wait and think.

Why was Brad popping into her mind now all of a sudden? It had been years. She had moved on.

Hadn't she?

Some things just weren't meant to be.

And some people could completely forget a goodbye kiss as sweet as theirs and start dating someone else ...

"Megan? Is that you?"

She jumped to her feet, hardly able to catch her breath. What was this, then? Some kind of cosmic practical joke?

"Brad?" It was really him. That same charming smile. The familiar intense gaze.

"What are you doing here?" they both asked at the same time.

Who would have thought that two people who met years ago in Vermont would find themselves in the same itsy bitsy small town in the middle of Washington's apple country?

"Do you have a minute?" Brad pointed to the chair next to hers.

"Oh. Sure. I mean, I'm waiting for someone. My sister-in-law. She just went to the bathroom. But yeah, have a seat." She was rambling, but she couldn't help it.

Brad sat down. "Did you say your sister-in-law?"

"Yeah. My brother's married and living here now. It was time for me to take my furlough, so I came here."

Strange how he'd hardly changed at all since she last saw him. She realized she was staring and tried to come up with something else to say. "What about you? I mean, what are you doing here?"

"This is where I grew up."

"Really?" She remembered he was from Washington, but Orchard Grove was such a small town. What were the chances?

"Yeah, I'm still working at the boys' home. I'm here on summer break. Are you still ..." He paused. "Are you still in Costa Rica?"

She nodded. "Yeah."

He leaned forward ever so slightly. "How's it going? I mean, are you enjoying the work there?"

"Uh-huh." She glanced at the bathroom. How long was Susannah going to take?

"How long will you be here for? Where are you staying?"

"I'm with my brother. I'll be here through the summer."

"Yeah? Who'd he marry? If she's from around town, maybe I know her."

"Her name's Susannah. I forget what her maiden name was."

His eyes widened. "So your brother's the missionary dude she met online. The two of them caused quite a stir. It was all my mom could talk about when an Orchard Grove girl got engaged to someone she met a few days earlier."

"They'd known each other long-distance for over a year by then," Megan asserted. When would people in this town learn to mind their own business?

He smiled. "Well, I'm sure they're great for each other." He lowered his gaze and cleared his throat. Megan rubbed her hands on her jeans and caught him staring at her finger. He glanced up, and their eyes met. She tried in vain to regain some sort of control over her breath.

"Thanks so much for waiting. I'm so sorry about that," Susannah apologized as she came out of the bathroom. She glanced over. "Oh, hi, Brad. I didn't know you were back in town."

He stood up. "Just here to see Grandma Lucy."

"Yeah? How's she doing?"

Megan wished she could telepathically communicate to Susannah that it was time to leave. Nothing good could come from her running into Brad here. Nothing but painful memories and more confusion.

As soon as he finished his quick run-down on Grandma Lucy's health, Megan butted in before Susannah could extend the conversation any further. "It's nice running into you. Maybe I'll see you around."

Something flashed in his eyes. Had she hurt his feelings? She ignored the guilt that pricked her conscience and forced herself to smile at her sister-in-law. "Ready?"

Susannah continued to seem totally oblivious to how uncomfortable Megan was. She said goodbye to Brad, and the two women walked back into the Orchard Grove heat.

Suddenly, Megan didn't feel like shopping at the farmer's market after all.

CHAPTER 23

Brad stared after Megan from the window of the bank. *God, you're going to have to let me know what you're doing here.*

Seeing her conjured up so many memories. Their ministry in Vermont had overlapped by only a few months, but it was enough time for him to see the love she had in her heart for the Lord, the passion she had to serve him. If she hadn't felt so called to the mission field in Costa Rica, she would have stayed in Vermont, and their relationship could have flourished and progressed.

Not that he hadn't tried. She didn't even know the lengths he'd gone to make their long-distance relationship work, but even that wasn't enough. She'd moved on.

He shook his head. At least she never found out how big a fool he'd made of himself.

He knew God had a plan for everything, even this apparently random meeting in the middle of nowhere, but couldn't God have given him some sort of warning? If Brad knew he'd bump into Megan Phillips here, he would have put on his anti-perspirant deodorant.

Oh, well. Too late for that now.

She was across the street, walking with Susannah toward the parking area. Would he see her again? Probably so. Orchard Grove was too small a town for people to stay anonymous. It was both the blessing and the curse of this place. In fact, chances were high they'd run into each other tomorrow at church at the latest.

He'd just have to remember his deodorant this time.

CHAPTER 24

"So how long after you broke up did he meet this other girl?" Susannah asked as they ate their ice cream sundaes under a little patio umbrella.

It had taken this long just to get the first part of the story out. Megan was surprised she'd shared so much already. Was the ice cream making her cold, or was there another reason her body kept shivering? She hoped Susannah didn't notice.

"Well, I'm not entirely sure we were ever officially dating. It was one of those weird things. I mean, we talked about our relationship when we were still working in Vermont, and we both recognized there was definitely some kind of romantic interest, but since I was headed to Costa Rica, I didn't think it was smart to pursue anything."

Susannah nodded and rubbed her pregnant belly.

Megan let out her breath. "And I guess that sounds all smart and logical, but I'm sure you know that's not really how romance works."

A smile spread across her sister-in-law's face.

"We tried to fight it, tried to convince ourselves we were nothing more than friends, friends who'd be saying goodbye in just a few weeks. But it was one of those cases where our brains were saying one thing, but our hearts were on a different page."

"I completely understand," Susannah admitted.

"So then I left for Costa Rica, and the night before I flew out we had this really perfect evening together and said goodbye, and then the next morning I woke up at three to hop on a plane to San Jose."

Her whole body felt heavy with the memories. "We emailed a lot at first. Even made plans for him to visit over Christmas break, and I thought things were going great."

Susannah paused with a spoonful of sundae halfway to her mouth. "What happened?"

Megan shrugged. "He never made it. I mean, that part wasn't his fault. He was supposed to fly out of Boston, and there was this major snowstorm, and it was one big mess. But then a few days later, he wrote and said that since God had called me to Costa Rica and him to Vermont, nothing would ever work out between us. Turns out he was dating one of the other counselors from the girls' home. And that was it."

"And how long ago was this?"

"Almost five years."

"Wow." Susannah glanced over her shoulder as if Brad might be there listening in on their conversation. "So was it strange seeing him again here?"

"Yeah."

Susannah grinned. "Think there's a chance of something developing now?"

Megan shook her head. The last thing she needed was for her mind to run wild through all the numerous *what ifs*. "I don't think so. I mean, I don't have plans to leave Costa Rica anytime soon, and if that was a deal-breaker for him then, it's still going to be now."

Susannah let out a little pout. "People change, you know."

Megan sighed. "Maybe. But I'm not looking for more confusion in my life. He kind of already showed me what sort of man he was, so in that case I'm glad things didn't progress between us."

Susannah nodded sympathetically. "I'm sorry."

The comment surprised her. "For what?"

Susannah shrugged. "For what you've gone through. I imagine it's lonely enough being on the mission field, even without the complications of a long-distance romance and all that. But you know, if he was ready to get over you that quickly and just start dating someone else again, maybe he's not worth getting so worked up over."

Yeah. How many times had Megan tried to tell herself that exact same thing when it happened?

Susannah scooted back her chair. "I'm so sorry."

Megan smiled. She was getting used to this by now. "Another bathroom break?"

Susannah set her sundae on the table. "I'll be back in a minute."

Megan watched her hurry off, then set her spoon in her half-eaten sundae and stared at the polka-dot pattern on the patio umbrella. She had forgotten until she started talking to Susannah how much Brad had hurt her by moving on as quickly as he had. Maybe she was still holding onto bitterness. Maybe that's what this strange run-in was all about. Maybe God was giving her a chance to fully forgive him for what he'd done.

All right, God, she prayed. *You've got my attention. I'm listening. Show me what you want me to do now.*

Maybe if she could get past the hurt and truly forgive Brad, she could finally heal.

Megan had never felt more ready to move on.

CHAPTER 25

"Did you have a nice run?" Mom asked when Brad returned home. His thoughts were so chaotic he'd ended up walking most of the way back just to give himself the extra time to think.

"Yeah," he answered. "Fine."

"Your father's in his den." Mom didn't say anything about their fight this morning, and Brad wasn't going to be the one to bring it up. "Okay."

She poured him a cup of iced tea and held it out.

"Thanks."

She studied him while he drank. "Is something wrong?"

"Like what?" he asked. Like the fact that he'd just run into Megan Phillips, a girl he hadn't seen in over four years? A girl he now realized he'd never fully gotten out of his heart, no matter how hard he tried to move on or give her the space that she needed?

Mom sighed. "I don't know, honey. But you feel so distant to me. You're all grown up now. It's like I hardly know you."

"Don't say that. We talk all the time."

"I know, but it's different on the phone than it is face to face."

That was for sure. That's why he had tried so hard to go visit Megan in Costa Rica, even though the snowstorm and the Boston airport and even God himself seemed to be barring the way for him so many years ago.

He handed his mom the empty glass. "Listen, I'm all sweaty and gross right now, but how about after I take a shower you show me whatever work you want me to do around the barn, or we can stay in here and have a snack or whatever you want, all right?" Anything was better than sitting alone upstairs in the attic wondering why God might have brought Megan into his life again.

Mom smiled. "All right. But don't be long. Grandma Lucy's got some medicine she needs to take, and I don't like her lying in bed all afternoon. She'll get sores."

Brad was already heading to the stairs. "All right. I'll be quick. Talk to you soon."

Yeah, a shower was exactly what he needed. A nice, hot shower to wash away his sweat and all his chaotic thoughts about this woman God had mysteriously brought back into his life.

CHAPTER 26

"Wait a minute." Scott's eyes flashed with anger. "You're talking about the same dude you spent that entire Christmas crying about?"

Susannah was in the bedroom, listening to *Odyssey* tapes with Kitty, and Megan hoped they couldn't overhear. "That's the one."

"And he's here in Orchard Grove?"

"Yeah. He told Susannah he was visiting his grandma."

Scott shook his head. "Want me to go over and beat him up for you? I will, you know."

Megan tried her best to match her brother's smile. "No. I was just wondering if you knew anything about him."

"I don't, but Susannah probably does. She knows everybody here. You should ask her. But wait, should I assume that you still have feelings for him after how terribly he treated you?"

"It wasn't all that bad."

Scott scoffed. "Oh, right. That's why I had to come fly

down to Costa Rica, and you spent just about every day between Christmas and New Year's crying because he'd dumped you for someone else?"

"That's not how it was."

"Well, it was something like that. I had to rearrange my whole travel plans. I was supposed to be in Moscow over Christmas and then fly to Johannesburg. Remember that? But you were so upset ..." Scott shook his head. "I can't believe that guy has the guts to show his face around here."

"It's not like he knew I'm here too. It was a total coincidence."

Scott sighed. "Well, I don't want you spending any time with him."

Even though seeing Brad again was the last thing Megan wanted to do, she bristled at her brother's attitude. She was too old for anyone to boss her around like that. But he was right, at least in principle. Sometimes it was nice having someone else looking out for her for a change.

Heaven knew their parents never had.

"I'm going to go lie down," she said.

He looked at her and frowned. "Are you sure you're okay?"

She nodded. "Yeah. I'm just tired from being up so late last night. So you think Kitty's going to be all right?"

He shrugged and lowered his voice. "Her fever's down, so that's good."

"Well, I hope she's getting some good rest."

Scott smiled. "Me too. Now you go do the same."

Megan got up. She'd never been more eager for a nap.

CHAPTER 27

"Grandma Lucy?" Brad gave her shoulder a gentle shake. "Grandma Lucy, it's time to wake up and take your medicine."

She muttered something in her sleep.

"What's she saying?" he asked his mom, who was standing by the door.

Mom shook her head. "I don't know. This is how it's been since that heart attack. One day she's fine, just as strong as ever, telling everybody she meets about Jesus and spending hours in her prayer chair talking to God, and the next she's like this, and you never know which it's going to be from one hour to the next."

"I still think you should talk to the doctor about that." Brad was no scientist, but it didn't seem normal that a woman as strong in spirit and sound in mind should be reduced to this kind of state. If his mother's assessment could be trusted, this wasn't like some sort of gradual decline that you could explain away with old age.

"We've been to the doctor," his mom reminded him. "He says it's most likely Alzheimer's and perfectly normal in someone that old. The medicine he prescribed is supposed to delay the symptoms a little bit, but there's really no cure."

"Yeah, but that was just the family doctor. You should take her to one of the specialists in Wenatchee or Spokane, don't you think?" Then again, what did he know? He just hated seeing Grandma Lucy like this.

Mom sighed. Brad didn't want to make her feel any worse. He knelt down by the bedside and called out in as gentle a voice as he could, "Grandma Lucy? Time to wake up."

Her eyes blinked open.

"You awake?" he asked, but his jocular tone was completely out of place when she looked at him with vacant eyes.

"The Lord has called you by name, and you are his," she mumbled. "Even though I walk through the valley of the shadow of death, I will fear no evil, for he is with me. His right arm is under me and his left hand sustains me. He awakens my soul like one being taught. At night his song is with me, a prayer to the God of my life."

She stared at the wall as if Brad weren't even in the room at all.

"His name is written on your forehead, and you're sealed with the Spirit of the Lord God Almighty."

"I know, Grandma. I know. Now let's sit you up so you can take your medicine."

She thrashed her head from side to side, and his mom ran her hand across Grandma Lucy's forehead. "What's wrong? What can we do for you?"

Grandma Lucy reached out and grabbed Brad's hand, holding on with an iron grip. "He has shown you, O man, what is good and what the Lord requires of you, but to love justice and mercy and to walk humbly with your God. For to obey the Lord is far more acceptable than sacrifice."

Brad looked at his mom. "What's she doing? What's she saying?"

Grandma Lucy was in the habit of quoting Scripture, had been breaking out into spontaneous prayer for as long as Brad had known her, but this felt different. Like she wasn't in control of her thoughts or her words. Nothing made sense.

"He will raise you up from this bed of sickness, and restore you to health. He rejoices over you with singing and crowns you with love and compassion so that your youth is renewed like the eagles."

It was a hodgepodge of biblical phrases and passages strung together that sounded more like nonsense than anything else. Brad looked at his mom. "Should we call the doctor or something?"

His mom shook her head, tears streaming down her cheeks. Great. Now he had two old women to worry about.

"Bless the Lord O my soul, and all my inmost being, bless his holy name." Grandma Lucy's voice rang out loud and clear, without any of the incoherent mumbling. "Bless the Lord O my soul and forget not all his benefits, who heals all my sicknesses and saves me from my infirmities. I was bent low and about to fall, but the Lord sustained me. I will bless the Lord as long as I live, and in his name I lift up my hands. My soul will be satisfied as with the richest of food, and with singing lips my mouth will praise him, for he has delivered my soul from death and my heart from fear and my feet from stumbling, that I may walk before the Lord in the land of the living. When I am afraid, I put my hope in him."

Brad couldn't tell if she was offering a prayer or a testimony or something that was a mix between the two, but her hands that held his had regained all the strength and vigor that he remembered from his younger days. "Grandma Lucy?"

A smile broke through her wrinkled face, and eyes that had once looked clouded over now stared at him calmly and clearly. "You have no idea how much better I feel now that you've prayed for me."

Brad didn't have the heart to tell her that he'd come to give her medicine, not to offer up any prayers.

His mother bent down and gushed. "Are you feeling better now, Grandma Lucy? You haven't seemed like yourself these past few days."

Grandma Lucy shook her head and sat up in bed as easily as if she had been Brad's age. "That devil's trying to convince me I'm old and infirm, but he doesn't know the power and strength of my Lord Jesus Christ."

Brad wasn't exactly sure what was going on. Was this just like what his mom said about how Grandma Lucy would sometimes have good days? Or was this something else? At first, when she started quoting all those Bible verses, he thought she was just mumbling a bunch of random thoughts that were floating through her head after years of Bible study and memorization. But maybe it was something else. She had claimed more than once that God had healed her from certain ailments. He didn't want to get his hopes up, didn't want to think that the cure for her recent mental confusion could come in the simple five-minute window of Scripture recitation, but more miraculous things than that had happened before, hadn't they?

"It's time for your medicine," he told her quietly.

Grandma Lucy waved her hand in the air dismissively, stood up from her bed, and walked on perfectly steady legs to the door before Brad caught up with her and took her elbow.

His mom came up on her other side, chiding, "You know you're not supposed to be walking without someone helping you. Should we get you your walker?"

Grandma Lucy shook her head. "The Lord says if the Son has set you free, you are free indeed. Now let's go into the kitchen. Man may not live on bread alone, but that doesn't mean I've got to starve in the middle of the day, does it?"

Brad kept his hold on Grandma Lucy's arm, even though her gait was perfectly steady and confident. He wanted to ask his mom what was going on, but they'd have to wait until they had some time alone together to talk.

The good news was that whether Grandma Lucy was truly healed from whatever mental fog had sapped her clarity or whether this was simply another facet of her illness, at least it had done one good thing.

It had gotten Brad's mind off Megan Phillips, if only for a few minutes.

CHAPTER 28

Even though she was tired after coming home from the Orchard Grove farmer's market, Megan hadn't expected to sleep so long. She woke up groggy and disoriented to find her brother shaking her gently by the shoulder and apologizing. "Megan, get up. We've got a problem."

His words were enough to make Megan jump up in bed. What was it? She rubbed her tired eyes and waited.

"It's Kitty," Scott explained. "Her fever's back up again, and she's having a really hard time breathing. Janice thinks we should probably take her to the ER to x-ray her lungs.

Megan battled through the sleepy fog that still hung heavily around her thoughts. "All right. So we're going to the ER?"

Scott nodded. "Susannah and I thought for a little bit that maybe we should just let you rest, but I worried you'd be upset if we left without you." He frowned apologetically. "I'm sorry you couldn't sleep any longer."

She glanced at the time. "It's no problem." It was

actually a good thing he had woken her up when he did, or else she would have an impossible time getting back to sleep tonight. "I can be ready in just a minute. Is Kitty okay? I mean, I know she's got that fever and stuff, but do you think it's really serious?"

She looked at her brother hopefully, the same way she had as a small child when she'd asked him if he thought dad would be angry when he came home from work. This time, however, her brother didn't try to shield her from the truth.

"With her body not responding to the antibiotics, and with as compromised as her lungs already are, it's pretty hard not to worry. Susannah's really upset."

"Are you sure you want me to tag along?" she asked as she got out of bed. "I don't want to be in the way or anything."

Scott shook his head. "No, come on. Susannah wants you there with her. She thinks you're absolutely adorable."

Megan smiled in spite of how tired and worried her brother looked. "Adorable? That's really what she said?"

Scott smiled softly. "Yes. Adorable."

CHAPTER 29

Orchard Grove County Hospital was only a few minutes away from the house. In fact, it took longer for Scott and Susannah to help Kitty into her wheelchair and then pack everything into the car than it did to actually make the drive. Susannah sat in the back seat, with Kitty's whole body resting against her. Several times Kitty made a quiet coughing sound, and Susannah would turn on the portable machine that suctioned out her throat.

Megan didn't know what to say. Growing up, Scott had always been the one looking out for her. Even when she first moved to Costa Rica, it was her brother who flew down to be with her when she was having such a hard time about her breakup with Brad. Not that you could call it a breakup since they hadn't technically been dating. Apparently, all those late-night conversations in Vermont, those lengthy emails when she first moved to Costa Rica meant nothing to him. Neither did their goodbye kiss. That was the only way to explain how he had moved on so quickly. She hated the way that she was still thinking about him, even now when Scott and Susannah clearly needed her. Not that Megan had any idea what she could do to actively help. Once they parked in front of the ER entrance, she watched her brother carefully pick Kitty up and set her in her wheelchair, wishing there was some way she could be involved. She offered up a prayer for Kitty's healing but had no idea how effective it would really be.

Once they got inside the hospital, the same young doctor was waiting for them in the hallway. She started asking about a dozen questions as Scott hurried Kitty to the exam room, and Megan trailed behind, hoping that God would show her a way to be an encouragement to her brother if only to make up for all the ways that he had looked out for her when they were little.

She didn't think back to those days at all if she could help it. Now that she was an adult, now that she no longer had any reason to subject herself to her father's explosive anger or her mother's infuriating inability to stand up to him, Megan did her best to go on with her life as if she'd never spent those seventeen years under their chaotic roof. Scott had been so afraid of leaving Megan alone when he went off to Bible college that he asked her best friend's parents to let her stay with them for her senior year of high school.

Even after he moved away, he was still watching out for her.

A nurse in Garfield scrubs was already waiting for them when they got to the room, and within minutes Kitty was hooked up to multiple monitors as well as an oxygen mask. Janice, the doctor, left to call Kitty's pulmonary specialist in Seattle for a phone consult, and the nurse started getting Kitty prepped for her first round of x-rays.

"You can't be in here for this, you know." Scott eyed his wife's belly. "Why don't you and Megan head to the waiting room, and I'll come and get you when they're done."

Susannah stood staring at her sister but didn't say anything. Scott wrapped his arms around her. "Come on, babe. She knows you're here for her, and you'll only be around the corner."

Susannah ran her hand lovingly across her sister's forehead and bent over to kiss her cheek. "Megan and I will be back in just a few minutes, okay? Don't give Scott or the nurse a hard time, you hear me?" There was teasing in her voice although her eyes betrayed the intensity of her worry.

Scott gave his wife's hand one last squeeze, and Megan followed Susannah out to the waiting room. "Are you holding up okay?" she asked once they'd found some seats. "Is there anything I can do to help?"

Susannah shook her head. "I know worrying is wrong, but I have no idea how in the world God expects me to stop. She's my sister."

"I know what you mean," Megan said. "When we were growing up, Scott was always the one worrying about me."

Susannah nodded sadly, and Megan went on. "The funny thing is he headed out to the mission field years before I did, and then I was the one worrying about him. He was all over the world. You know how things were before you guys got married, and it was almost a full-time job just keeping up with every place he went so I could be praying for him. It's strange now because I think once we both became adults, it was sort of like our roles reversed, and I was the mature one, and he was out traveling the world. And now he's finally settled down here with you, and it's weird," she concluded lamely. "How quickly things change, you know?"

Susannah sighed. "It's almost the opposite with Kitty," she confessed. "Her condition really hasn't changed at all for as long as I can remember. And that's not a bad thing because it means she hasn't been getting worse, at least not until recently. I've known from the time I was pretty young that someday it would be my responsibility to take care of her, but I have to admit I feel like I'm doing a pretty horrible job." Susannah's chin quivered.

"You shouldn't say that. You're doing amazing. I just got here, and I can already see how devoted you are."

Susannah shook her head. "She didn't get this sick when Mom was still alive. Mom hated antibiotics. Only used them if it were literally a life-and-death situation." She let out a heartless sounding chuckle. "I guess she was right."

"You can't go blaming yourself." Megan packed certainty and confidence into her voice. "This is probably just what would have happened no matter who was taking care of Kitty, right?"

Susannah shrugged. There was no real way to answer the question. Megan knew that.

There was no way to guess all the hypotheticals.

Like what if Brad had started working at the boys' home just a few weeks earlier, before Megan signed a contract with the Kingdom Builders mission in Costa Rica? What if there hadn't been that snowstorm, and they'd actually gotten to spend her first Christmas down there together like they first planned?

It was senseless to think through these kinds of questions. It wouldn't help her, and it would do absolutely nothing to encourage her sister-in-law.

"How long do the x-rays usually take?"

Susannah sighed and glanced at the clock on the wall.

"We'll probably have to wait a while. It's hard to get Kitty to understand that she has to stay perfectly still."

"I'm guessing you wish you could be with her, don't you?" Megan asked softly.

Susannah gave a slight nod. "It's hard because in a way I've been taking care of my sister my entire life. Obviously more so in the past year since Mom died, but even before that I was always involved in her care. And now I have this little one." She looked down and rubbed her belly. "And as a mom I know I'm supposed to make him or her my ultimate priority, but sometimes I just feel angry that I can't be there for Kitty when she needs me. That's probably a terrible thing for me to say, isn't it?"

"No. I'm sure that's perfectly natural. And trust me, when the baby comes, God's going to give you the strength to take care of both them and your sister. It will all be just fine, you'll see."

Even as the words came out of her mouth, Megan prayed that she was speaking the truth.

CHAPTER 30

"So you're feeling totally better then?" Brad asked.

Grandma Lucy leaned back in the rocking chair in her prayer room and laughed. "I told you, the devil just wanted to keep me weak and confused, probably so I couldn't spend as much time in prayer as I normally do. But what that old fox doesn't know is that my Lord has conquered death, hell, and the grave, and I have the blood of Jesus poured out over my soul, and God has not promised me a spirit of fear but of power and love and a sound mind. So that devil can just take his tricks and his mischief straight on out of here."

Brad tried to smile. Tried to share Grandma Lucy's confidence, but all he could think about was the way she had looked at him earlier and hadn't even known who he was. Mom said the dementia symptoms came and went. Was this afternoon of clarity divine healing like Grandma Lucy claimed, or was it just part of the Alzheimer's progression, a short reprieve before confusion reigned once more?

She wagged a finger at him slyly. "You're just like

Thomas, aren't you?"

"Who?" Brad had dozens of cousins, many of whom he'd only met once or twice. How was he expected to keep track of them all like she did?

"The apostle Thomas," Grandma Lucy explained. "The one who refused to believe until he touched Jesus' hands and side himself. After he saw Jesus, he was just as faithful as the Lord's brother James. They called James Camel Knees. Did I ever tell you why?"

"No, why?"

"Because after he was saved, he spent so much time on his knees, they got knobby and ended up resembling a camel's more than a man's." She looked down at her lap and laughed again. "Looks like I haven't done as well as James did, have I? It's a good thing I'm under grace, or my sweet Savior might end up disappointed in me for not being as faithful in prayer as I should be."

Brad was convinced that there was nobody alive who prayed as much as she did, but he knew if he said so she would just offer her humble protests.

"Well, I'm glad you're feeling better." That much was true at least. Whether or not she was cured as she claimed or was just experiencing a reprieve from the dementia symptoms, this afternoon was a blessing from the Lord either way.

"Now tell me." Grandma Lucy leaned forward in her rocker and set her hands on Brad's shoulders. "Why do you look so troubled, and how can I bless you more thoroughly with my prayers?"

Her gaze was so intense he ended up looking at a spot just past her shoulder.

"Oh, I'm all right," he answered. "I was just worried about you. That's all."

She leveled her gaze directly at him until his palms began to sweat. "Then you shall know the truth, and the truth shall set you free."

Great. She was back to quoting Scripture again. Before he could say anything else, she began to pray.

"Lord God, awesome Creator of the entire universe, you know exactly what this son of yours needs for life and peace and godliness. You know exactly what lies he has bought into and how those lies have trapped him in bondage. Heavenly Father, you are not a God of confusion but of unity and love and power, and today I speak truth over this servant of yours. Open his eyes that he can see the wonderful plans you have in store for him. Open his mind so he can understand the spiritual battle that right now wages war against his soul. Strengthen him as a mighty soldier for your kingdom until he is no longer just a man doing mission work to serve his God but a front-line soldier confronting the powers of darkness as he does battle for you, the King of kings and Lord of lords who alone reigns supreme over the entire universe.

"I declare that no weapon forged against him today shall prevail. I declare that when his enemies attack him, they will flee and scatter in every direction in submission to the mighty name of Jesus, who surrounds and protects his children with the power of his love. Only you know the longings in his soul. Only you know the secret sins he's entertained."

Brad's hands clammed up even more. It was one thing to sit here while Grandma Lucy prayed blessings over him and his ministry, but it was quite another to hear her talking about his secret sins. Just what kind of stuff did she suspect he was involved in?

"Hear his prayer, Father God, and restore every broken relationship."

Great. This was the part where her prayer turned into a thinly veiled sermon, and she made him feel guilty for not having a better relationship with his father. Did she think he hadn't tried?

"You are the God who gives and takes away, and you are

the God who blesses every single sacrifice that we offer up to you. This child of yours has been serving you faithfully his whole life, sharing your word with those teenagers who are desperate to know your truth. He has given up so much, dear Lord, more than perhaps he's even admitted to himself, but you know and you see and you are delighted with his sacrifice, and I know that you will continue to strengthen him for the work that you have called him to do until he will have everything he needs, being thoroughly equipped for every good work which he was created by you in advance to accomplish. I declare today that your purposes for him shall not fail, that the destiny you have designed for him shall come to pass, and the darkness will no longer reign in his mind or in his heart or in his soul because all of these belong to you and are protected by the precious blood of Jesus Christ, the Lamb of God who washes away the sins of the world.

"I speak victory today over your precious servant. Victory to serve you and please you and honor you in everything he does, and I know that your purposes for him shall not fail."

She hadn't closed her eyes but had been staring at him during her entire prayer. It wasn't until she finished that he was able to meet her gaze. Before he could thank her for the blessing of her intercession, she took his hand in hers and said, "Well now, do you think your mom's finished getting our snack ready? I wonder if she knows I'm sitting here about to starve?"

CHAPTER 31

"So you really think she needs to stay here tonight?" Susannah asked the doctor in a quiet voice.

Megan stood back, feeling out of place while the conversation unfolded.

Janice nodded. "I'm so sorry. I hate to get you worried like this, but until we find something to help her clear out her lungs, I'm really not comfortable sending her home."

"What about oxygen?" Scott questioned. "Last month we were able to get those two canisters of oxygen to keep on her at home, and I think that really helped. Could we do something like that again?"

Janice shook her head. "I wouldn't recommend it. Until we find some antibiotics she's not resistant to, I really think she's going to need more supervision. Not that you guys aren't doing a great job. I just want to make sure she's getting all the attention she needs. I want to put her on IVs since she's here too."

Scott looked at his wife. "Does that sound okay?"

Susannah sighed heavily. "I guess so. I suppose I should give you a list of things to grab from the house to throw into my overnight bag ..."

Scott shook his head. "No. You're not spending the night here." He hurried on before Susannah could interrupt. "Listen. You're pregnant. You need all the sleep you can get, and there's nothing you can do for Kitty that the nurses can't."

"You know how she gets," Susannah argued. "She'll be terrified."

"That's why I'm staying the night. Don't bother arguing. You can take first shift and spend the rest of the afternoon and evening here. You'll do a better job answering any of the intake questions and filling out all the history forms and everything else anyway. And that's when Kitty's going to need you most, when she's awake, right?"

"I suppose," Susannah answered tentatively.

Janice excused herself to make a phone call, and Megan stood feeling dumb and useless while her brother and his wife made their plans.

"You stay here now so when she wakes up from her nap, you can help her calm down and feel relaxed, and then I'll come over tonight, and we can trade places."

"I'm really not sure ..." Susannah glanced at Megan,

who wasn't about to step into the middle of their dispute. Apparently sensing the battle was already lost, Susannah sighed. "All right. If that's how you want to do it. I guess that makes the most sense."

Scott nodded. "Do you want us all to stick around a little bit more, or are you ready for some alone time with your sister?"

Susannah turned toward Kitty's room. "I'll be fine." She forced a timid smile. "I know Megan didn't come all this way just to watch us sitting around a hospital room."

"I'll do whatever's best for you guys and Kitty," Megan was quick to assert.

Scott leaned over to hug his wife. "Think about anything you or Kitty might want me to bring from home. I'll take Megan back now, and we'll stop back in later this evening. I'll show Megan a little bit around town, give her the grand tour of Orchard Grove." He smiled gallantly. "You gonna be okay?" He squeezed Susannah's hand. "Just hang in there. It's good that you'll be here when Kitty wakes up."

Susannah nodded. Her expression was still pained, but she gave Megan a smile. "Enjoy your tour. I'm sorry I'm not a better hostess for you today."

Megan refused to be one more thing for Susannah to worry about. "This is totally fine. I want to be as helpful as I can. If you and Scott want some time at the hospital alone, that's cool too. I can make my way back to the house and come by later. It's whatever you all need. And what's best for Kitty."

"You should go with Scott," Susannah told her. "He's been dying to show you around town anyway, and all you've seen so far is the inside of a bank and an ice cream shop. Go have fun. I'll see you both later tonight."

"Wait a minute." Scott said. "Before we all spread out, let's go in and pray for Kitty. How's that sound?"

Susannah nodded, and Megan wondered how her brother had read her mind.

"That sounds like a great idea," she told him, and the three of them went into Kitty's room to pray.

CHAPTER 32

"So that's when I told him, *Son, Jesus Christ is the only one who can forgive your sins, and getting those ridiculous tattoos is just your soul's way of crying out for healing that can only come from the blood of the precious Lamb of God.*"

Grandma Lucy set down her cup of tea and chuckled.

"You really said that?" Brad asked. "Right there in front of everybody?"

"Oh, yeah. We were all there, me, your mom, your cousin Jillian, and quite a few others, too. We had gone out for a quick lunch if I remember right, and I'll tell you, that waiter's never going to forget serving our table."

"I guess not. Did you hear from him again?"

"Sure did," Grandma Lucy answered. "Next Sunday he came to church just like I told him to. That afternoon we had him over for lunch, led him in the sinner's prayer, and now he and his sister and her kids are all baptized, born-again believers. All because I had such a strong hankering for fried chicken one afternoon."

Brad might have a hard time believing Grandma Lucy's story if he hadn't grown up with her witnessing like this to random strangers and seeing such immediate results on a regular basis. He wondered if he would have even thought to go into full-time ministry if it hadn't been for the example she set when he was young.

"What about you?" Grandma Lucy asked.

"Me what?"

"Tell me about the teens you minister to in Vermont. Have you seen many saved lately?"

"It's a little more complicated than that," he replied. The teens at the boys' home came from broken families. Many were ordered there as an alternative to juvenile detention centers. Grandma Lucy had to understand what kind of people he was working with. These weren't prodigals who grew up in church and made a few wrong choices along the way.

She crossed her arms. "Well, if you're not seeing God move, you need to pray for revival. Are you and the workers there fasting regularly? How much time do you set aside each day to pray?"

He wished he could tell her that not everyone saw immediate spiritual results with their witnessing efforts like she did. There wasn't some kind of formula that would guarantee success. Besides, how would you even go about measuring success at something like the boys' home anyway? Some things you just had to accept by faith whether or not you saw results from your efforts.

"And what about girls?" Grandma asked. "Has the Lord brought anybody special into your life?

"I haven't dated anyone in a while."

"Wasn't there a nice young woman working at the girls' home you were seeing?"

He sighed. "Yeah, but it didn't work out." As glad as he was that Grandma Lucy's memory seemed completely functional, that didn't mean he wanted to sit here while she pried into the past five years of his personal life.

He was thankful when Mom walked in through the back door after checking on all the farm animals. "How are you feeling, Grandma?" she asked. "Still doing well?"

"This old soul of mine is just as strong as ever. Here, let me help you with that basket of eggs. They're about to spill.

"No, Grandma, I'll get them." Brad stood too, but Grandma Lucy was up first.

"I'm not an invalid. Let me help."

"No, Grandma," Brad repeated. "I've got it."

Grandma Lucy shook her head. "Nonsense. Just because I was laid up a few days and not my full self, that's no reason to treat me like a cripple." She reached out for the basket of eggs but lost her balance. Brad managed to snatch his hand out and grab her by the elbow, but gravity and momentum were both working against him.

Grandma Lucy let out a small cry as she fell forward. Her head hit the side of the table with a dull thud, and she landed on the floor, surrounded by egg yolks, broken shells, and a growing puddle of blood.

CHAPTER 33

Megan had almost forgotten how nice it was to pray for somebody in English. She was fluent in Spanish and never thought twice about using it, but being back in the States reminded her how much mental energy it takes to converse day in and day out in a second language.

Their prayer time with Kitty was powerful and touching. Susannah started to cry toward the end, and Megan had stepped out so she and Scott could be alone with Kitty for a few minutes. Maybe it hadn't been the best time for her to fly out to Washington after all. Then again, if there was anything she could do to make things easier for Scott and Susannah while she was here, it was worth it.

After all the ways her brother had shielded her from their father's wrath growing up, this was one of the smallest things she could do in hopes of repaying him.

She sat in the hospital lobby, her heart full and heavy at the same time. At first, she had figured Susannah and Scott must be used to frequent hospital visits, but she could tell based on how upset her sister-in-law was that this was a much more serious illness than usual, even if Susannah joked that her tears were the result of pregnancy hormones more than anything.

Megan was glancing at the photographs on the walls of the waiting room when a buzzer sounded and the sliding doors opened automatically.

She glanced up.

"Brad?"

He ran to the reception area, hardly acknowledging her. "It's Grandma Lucy," he told the triage nurse. "She fell and hit her head. She's bleeding. I need someone to help me get her in."

Megan watched, feeling just as helpless as she had witnessing Scott and Susannah's worry over Kitty. Brad rushed two hospital workers outside, and they came back a minute later, pushing a white-haired old woman in a wheelchair.

"I'm telling you it was just a silly little accident." She held a rag up to her forehead. "I don't need doctors poking and prodding me everywhere. Just a little something for the bleeding."

"I still want them to check you out all over," Brad told her.

Megan sat in her seat, feeling even more awkward than she had in Kitty's hospital room. Would there ever be a moment during her time here in Orchard Grove where she didn't feel terribly out of place?

Brad followed the hospital workers, and they all disappeared down the hallway.

Scott came out just a few breaths later. "Ready to go?" he asked.

Megan blinked. What had just happened?

"You ready?" Scott repeated.

She stood up. "Yeah. How's Susannah? Is she okay?"

He nodded. "It's hard seeing her sister like this, but she's a strong one."

"I can tell."

He cocked his head to the side, studying her. "How about you? Are you all right?"

"Yeah." She cleared her throat. "Yeah, I'm just starting to get a little hungry." She another glance past her brother's shoulder to see if she might see Brad or his grandmother one more time.

Scott smiled. "Well, it's just about dinnertime. How do you feel about picking up some burgers?"

CHAPTER 34

"It's kind of nice having dinner together, just the two of us, isn't it?" Scott asked with his mouth full.

Megan nodded. "Yeah."

He chomped on several fries at once. "You and Susannah seem to be getting along well. Did you have fun with her this morning?"

"She's great. I just feel bad to be here with Kitty so sick and all."

Scott didn't respond.

"I'm happy to help out if I can," she added. "Can you think of anything I could do?"

He drenched his burger in more ketchup. "It's just nice having you here. Like I said, there's not too many women Susannah's age around town that she gets together with or anything."

Megan stared at her plate. "How long do you think Kitty will have to stay at the hospital?"

Scott sighed. "Based on how bad things got last time, it'll

be at least several days. Maybe longer if they don't find antibiotics that will work."

She could sense he didn't want to talk through the situation. She doubted there was much more she could say or ask about Kitty's medical condition that wouldn't end up being more discouraging than helpful. There had to be something else they could talk about.

"I saw Brad at the hospital." She watched while her brother took a huge bite from his burger. When he didn't say anything, she tried to find a way to fill the silence. "There was something wrong with his grandma. She had fallen and hit her head. I'm not sure how serious it was."

"That was Grandma Lucy. I saw them bringing her into the ER. She had a heart attack last spring, and now they say she's suffering some dementia."

"That's too bad." What else was there to add?

"Weird seeing him?" Scott asked after an uncomfortable silence.

"Yeah, I guess so. I mean, we didn't say anything. I was just there while they wheeled his grandma in. That's all."

Scott wiped his mouth with his napkin. "Well, you know how I feel about him. Anybody who would just leave you there in Costa Rica by yourself and not even have the guts to tell you he'd found someone else … Well, as much as I love

Grandma Lucy, I'm not a very big fan of this Brad dude. Hope it doesn't hurt your feelings to hear me say that."

She would never admit it, but it felt nice to have her brother acting so protectively again.

"Why do you call her Grandma Lucy?" she asked. No reason to talk about Brad any more than they had to.

"That's what everyone in town calls her. Even her niece Connie, the one she lives with. You'd have to ask Susannah to be sure, but I'm guessing that guy you know and keep running into is Connie's son. I heard something about him doing some teaching at a Christian school out East. I just never thought to put two and two together and realize he was the same jerk who broke your heart all those Christmases ago."

"He didn't break my heart." Megan couldn't quite meet her brother's gaze.

"What do you call it when you can't even get through Christmas dinner without crying?"

There was no use denying it. She'd have to just recite some of the excuses she'd been telling herself for years. "I was young. He was the first guy I'd ever been all that interested in."

"Well, what about since then? Should I start introducing you to all my Spanish-speaking single missionary friends?"

He was joking, so she didn't bother to respond but stared out the window. The sun would be setting soon. Where had the day gone?

"You're still thinking about him, aren't you?"

She snapped her attention back to her brother. "What? No, I'm not."

He grinned. "Yes, you are. You want me to get more information about him from Susannah? Want me to come up with all the reasons why you should forget you ever knew him?"

"You don't have to do that."

Scott's features softened. "Hey, you know I'm just teasing you, right?"

"Yeah, I know."

"Because if you really thought this was somebody worth getting reacquainted with, it's not like there's a whole lot on the agenda over the next few days."

She shook her head. "You and Susannah are both going to be really busy with Kitty, and I came out here to spend time with you, not some random guy I met years ago."

Some random guy. That's what she'd have to keep telling herself he was. Some random guy she'd kissed the night before she moved to Costa Rica. Some random guy she'd given her affection to foolishly no matter how undeserving he was.

Some random guy who still made her heart flutter like a schoolgirl's every time she gave him a passing thought.

CHAPTER 35

"And that's why Jesus came to die on the cross, to take away the punishment for our sins," Grandma Lucy told the nurse in the Garfield scrubs who was getting ready to start her stitches.

Brad excused himself. He had never been too comfortable with needles, and Grandma Lucy seemed to be doing just fine without him. County was a small hospital, but he raced down the hallway as fast as he'd start his morning jog.

He had to find Megan.

It was probably silly for him to get this worked up about a girl who had hurt him so deeply, but that was all in the past. People could change, couldn't they? Brad thought about the time he and Megan spent together the night before she left Vermont to head to that school in Costa Rica. She was the first girl he had ever kissed. But apparently, their time together had meant far more to him than it had to her. He still burned with shame when he thought about how far he had traveled just to be with her.

And all for nothing.

That was years ago. Four and a half to be exact. Everybody deserved a second chance, didn't they? Everybody needed forgiveness, like that nurse who was probably right now hearing the gospel message from Grandma Lucy.

Nobody was perfect. Brad certainly wasn't, or he would have been more forthcoming about his feelings for Megan before she even left for Costa Rica. At the time, he had thought he was doing the right thing by not tying her down when she was so clearly called to the mission field. He didn't want to stand in her way, and foolishly he had assumed that even with the long distance, they could continue to grow their relationship.

She couldn't even wait a full two months from the time of their first and ultimately last kiss before finding someone else. He wondered whatever happened to that other dude she'd been with.

Well, it didn't matter. Besides, he was the one who'd been too stupid to ask Megan to be his official girlfriend before she moved away. He had assumed like a fool that the kiss they shared her last night in Vermont meant that they wouldn't date anybody else. You really had to spell things out these days, didn't you?

Well, whether or not she still had any sort of feelings toward him, it would be rude to run into someone he knew after all these years and not make at least a little bit of an effort to reconnect.

On a purely platonic level.

That's what he kept telling himself as he sprinted down the hospital corridor. And if God had something else in store, maybe this time Brad would have the courage to speak his mind before it was too late.

Before he found her in someone else's arms again.

He raced into the lobby, a hundred different questions for her swarming in his head.

When he got into the waiting room, she was gone.

CHAPTER 36

Scott grabbed a can of Diet Coke from the fridge after he finished talking to his wife.

"What did Susannah say?" Megan asked. "How's Kitty doing?"

He popped the can open. "She's still having a hard time keeping her oxygen levels up. They're doing their best to keep her stable, but I guess there's talk of transferring her to Seattle if her numbers keep dropping."

Scott sighed and sat down at the dining room table. "How are you holding up? I suppose this isn't exactly what you signed up for when you flew out here."

Megan just wished she could stop feeling so guilty. If she weren't here visiting, Scott would probably be at the hospital with Susannah. He could be there to lend her the support she needed.

"I'm fine," she answered. "I just worry about you. It's got to be a lot of stress."

She stared at her brother, wondering when he had gotten

those wrinkles across his brow.

Scott took a noisy gulp of soda. "I guess that's kind of like me saying you must get really stressed out working in Costa Rica, know what I mean? For you, it's a demanding job, and I'm sure it's spiritually and physically draining at times, but it doesn't matter all that much if you're serving where God has called you." He leveled his gaze. "You still feel called to be there, don't you?"

Megan nodded emphatically. Of course she was called to work in Costa Rica. Why else would she have devoted the past four and a half years of her life there?

"Are you sure?"

"Yes, I'm sure. Why are you staring at me like that?" An uneasy flutter started in the base of her gut.

Scott let out a sigh. "It's just that when I met Susannah, one of the biggest things keeping us apart at first was that I was called to the mission field, and we didn't see how that was going to work when she had to stay here in Orchard Grove to take care of Kitty. One of my buddies back at the home office, he's convinced that I've sold out or missed God's plans for my life because I'm not traveling around the world fifty weeks out of every year like I use to."

"That's ridiculous," Megan huffed. When had Christians become so judgmental? "You're doing amazing work for the

Lord right where you are."

"I know, but some people don't see it that way. If we're going to be totally honest with each other, I struggled with it some too. I still struggle. People here ask me what I do, and I've stopped telling them I'm a missionary because it doesn't make sense to them that a missionary could be living full time in their own little quiet town. So I say I work from home for a Christian organization, and the truth of the matter is that's not quite as glamorous a title as *missionary*."

"But you've got Susannah, and you've got your baby coming ..."

"Oh," Scott interrupted, "I wouldn't trade any of this for all the fancy titles in the world. What I'm saying is I'm glad that I didn't let this whole idea that God called me to be a missionary stop me from marrying the woman of my dreams and settling down and serving him here in any way I can."

What was he saying? Was he starting to lecture her? Did he doubt that God wanted her in Costa Rica?

"So you're suggesting it was wrong for me to leave Vermont?"

Great. Her own brother — the one who had been her biggest source of comfort and support when her relationship with Brad deteriorated — was convinced she had moved down to Costa Rica and sacrificed everything that was dear to her because she was vain and thought it sounded glamorous.

Scott shook his head. "I'm not saying that at all." He let out his breath. "I'm sorry. I don't even know what I'm saying. I've just been rambling. These are things I've been thinking about and dealing with myself. I shouldn't be projecting all of this on you or burdening you with it."

"It's not a burden." When had her brother stopped thinking he could share anything with her? "I didn't mean to sound upset, either. It's just that you brought up Susannah and how you didn't regret changing your plans so you could start your family here, and I thought you were telling me I made a mistake when I left Vermont."

Scott's eyes widened. "What? No. That's not what I meant. I was talking about me. It's something I've been asking myself. You remember how things were for us growing up. And yeah, I definitely know that God called me to the mission field. But the fact that by becoming a missionary I'd end up thousands of miles away from the man who hurt us so much and the woman who refused to stop him certainly made the decision easier."

She blinked at her brother. For all they shared with one another throughout the years, they hardly ever brought up their childhood.

Scott drummed his fingers on his soda can. "Like I said, this is just stuff that God's been working on in me. I have no idea how or if it applies to you. And I certainly don't want to make you doubt all the work you've done in Costa Rica. You should hear how the Central America director back in the home office raves about your team. I'm serious. That school and the orphanage are like the Kingdom Builders' Central American trophy. You've done an outstanding job, and I know you went there because God called you to. So don't listen to me. I'm just blabbering on about things that don't really matter and don't make an ounce of sense. I'm going to go grab those few things Susannah asked me to take to the hospital. Want to come along for the ride?"

"Sure."

"You're not too tired?"

"No. And hey, I'm sure you and Susannah could use some time alone together with Kitty. What if I drop you off so you all can be together for a little bit?"

He frowned at her. "That might be nice. If you're sure you're not going to feel too put out."

"Not at all. I might drive myself around town some. See what's here."

"I guess we didn't end up getting much of a tour after dinner, did we?"

143

"No, but that's fine. You know me. I don't mind traveling by myself." What else did he think she'd done for the past four and a half years?

"All right. Hey, are you upset? Were you offended when we were talking earlier?"

Megan shook her head. "No, I wasn't offended." That much was the truth, but what she didn't admit was how her brother's words had planted seeds of doubt in a mind already plagued with far too many questions and far too few answers.

CHAPTER 37

She was gone. Stupid for Brad to think otherwise. What had he expected, for Megan to just sit around in the hospital waiting for him to show up? Why was she here, anyway? And what would she think after the way he just barged through the lobby, totally ignoring her ...

Now she was gone.

It was just like that stupid last-minute flight he'd taken to Costa Rica to see her.

At first, they both joked that maybe God didn't want them to see each other over Christmas. It certainly felt as if there was some sort of divine interference. The snowstorm that covered New England broke several decades-old records. When they talked by phone, they agreed that it would be best for Brad to wait until his summer break to try again. That way he wouldn't have to take any time off teaching at the boys' home.

But in the end, he decided he wouldn't wait that long. He couldn't. The airline worker he spoke with must have sensed his desperation and charged him nearly double the price of the original ticket to fly out sooner. It was going to be a surprise, a Christmas present to this woman he had grown to admire so much. He didn't want to admit it even to himself at the time, but he was also praying that God would use this trip to show him if he was being led to ministry in Costa Rica. To serve by Megan's side.

He should have left it alone. Should have taken the snowstorm as the warning flag it was. Some things just weren't meant to be. Megan had realized that before he had, which explained how she moved on so quickly.

He shook his head. Some things wouldn't change. She hadn't waited for him all those years ago, and she hadn't waited for him now. Why should she? She was her own free person. Free to do whatever it was she wanted.

Although it would be nice to get the chance to talk to her since they happened to be spending their summers stuck in this same little town. He could ask her how she was doing, if she still liked her work at the school in Costa Rica, if she still thought about the night they kissed …

He shook his head. Maybe this was all God's doing. Maybe God was protecting him now like he had back then, sending multiple red flags his way. There was nothing good that could come from trying to pursue any sort of relationship with someone like her.

He should have listened years ago when God sent that snowstorm.

Well, this time he wasn't going to be nearly so stubborn.

CHAPTER 38

"And the Bible tells us in the book of 1 John that *if we confess our sins, he is faithful and just and will forgive us our sins and purify us from all unrighteousness.*" Grandma Lucy sat in her wheelchair and beamed at Ruby in her Garfield scrubs. "That promise is for all of us, no matter how sinful we are or how hard it is for us to believe that God could ever accept someone so unworthy. There's nothing you can do to stop God from loving you, nothing you have done that he's not ready and willing to forgive, right here, right now."

The nurse Ruby glanced over when Brad came into the room. Mascara streaked down her cheeks.

Grandma Lucy took her hand in hers. "Shall I pray for you? Would you like to accept this wonderful gift of grace and forgiveness that Jesus offers?"

Ruby nodded.

Incredible. How did Grandma Lucy do it?

Brad listened while Grandma Lucy prayed for her most

recent convert and wondered how many hundreds of people were saved as a direct result of her witness.

Would he ever have a testimony like that? The irony was that he worked in full-time ministry, and Grandma Lucy had been retired for as long as Brad had been alive. Yet here she was, sharing the gospel with the nurse who'd stitched up her forehead, praying while God ushered a new soul into his kingdom while the angels rejoiced.

Incredible.

He thought Ruby might be embarrassed, but when she opened her eyes after Grandma Lucy's prayer, her entire face was shining. She smiled at him. "Come in. Your grandma just prayed for me."

"I know. That's the kind of thing she does."

Ruby beamed. "I've never felt like this before. It's like I've been wondering my entire life if I really have a purpose, if there's any reason why I'm here. And now I know." She reached down and hugged Grandma Lucy. "Thank you so much."

Grandma Lucy took her hand. "Remember, this is only the beginning. It's God's grace that saves you and makes you acceptable to him, but it's your turn now to take that free gift he's given you and work out the salvation he's so generously offered."

"How do I do that?"

Brad glanced at the time. At this rate, they'd be here until midnight.

"Do you have a Bible?" Grandma Lucy was already rummaging through her purse.

"I don't know. I think I could probably find something online."

Grandma Lucy shook her head. "No, no. That won't do at all. You take this. I always carry an extra just in case." She handed Ruby a small paperback New Testament. "You start tonight, as soon as your shift's over. You go home and you read a chapter or two from the book of John. It will tell you all about Jesus and what he did for you."

"That's it?"

Grandma Lucy chuckled. "No. But it's a start. Oh, and you'll come join us for church tomorrow. Do you know where Orchard Grove Bible is?"

Ruby nodded.

"Services start at 10:30, so we'll see you there. And one more thing."

"Yeah?"

"I want you to pray tonight and ask God who he wants you to tell about this wonderful gift of salvation he's given you. It's a message that's meant to be shared, you know."

At this point, Brad was certain Ruby would balk or come up with some sort of excuse, but she just nodded and gave Grandma Lucy one last hug.

"I'm so glad you came in tonight. I mean, I'm sorry you needed stitches, but I've literally been searching the web trying to figure out what I'm supposed to do with my life and if there's any real reason why I'm here. This is the first time I've felt so much hope and joy. More than I can remember in my entire life."

Grandma Lucy smiled. "Bless you, child. And I'm going to add you to my prayer book, and you just remember that for as long as God keeps me alive, I'm going to be praying for you every single day, asking God to fan into flame the Spirit he's placed within you, asking him to make you grow in the knowledge and grace of our Lord and Savior Jesus, asking him to fill you in Christ with every spiritual blessing so that you'll become more than a conqueror through him who loved you and gave himself up for you."

"I appreciate that so much. I don't know if any Christian's ever prayed for me before."

"Well, now you'll have at least one." Grandma smiled and cleared her throat. "There's just a small favor I need to ask you before you head out."

"Anything."

If Brad didn't know Grandma Lucy better, he would have said there was a hint of embarrassment in her eyes. "I need you to tell me your name one more time so I can add it to my prayer list. I'm afraid I've already forgotten it."

CHAPTER 39

Brad walked into the kitchen where his mom was sweeping the floor. "Grandma Lucy's down for the night."

She smiled. "Good. It's been quite the adventurous day for you, hasn't it?"

"Something like that," he replied.

"Would you like some iced tea?" She held out a glass.

Brad pulled out a chair. "Need a hand with anything?" he asked before he sat down.

"No, just finishing up in here. Why don't you keep me company for a little bit, and when I'm done we can go tuck the animals in for the night."

"Okay." Brad knew he could never move back to Orchard Grove long-term, but there was something comforting about the thought of a nice, relaxing summer here. Helping out around the farm when he was needed, going on his morning runs. There was definitely something to be said in favor of a missionary's furlough. He'd die of boredom if he had to stay in Orchard Grove for good, but for a few months, he could get used to this.

Especially if Grandma Lucy stayed away from the emergency room from now on.

"What are you thinking about, honey?"

He hadn't realized his mom was staring at him. "Nothing really."

"Come on. You can tell me."

"Seriously," he insisted, "I wasn't thinking about anything."

"No? What about that nurse Grandma Lucy witnessed to tonight at the hospital?"

"Why would I be thinking about her?"

"Grandma Lucy said she was pretty."

Brad rolled his eyes.

"I'm not trying to pry," Mom said. "I just want to see you happy."

He didn't respond.

She handed him a stack of mail. "If you're not doing anything else, would you go take this in to your father?"

"Sure." Brad stood up with a sigh. Why were his legs so achy? He made his way slowly to the den.

"Come in," Dad called when Brad knocked on the door. He looked up from his newspaper.

Brad set the envelopes on his father's desk. "Mom

wanted me to bring this in."

"Yeah? How's Grandma Lucy? She doing all right?"

It was the first conversation of the day that wasn't about how lazy Brad was or inconsiderate for staying away from home for so long.

"She's asleep now. The cut wasn't really that deep."

His dad let out a low mumble, and Brad turned to leave.

"Wait."

He stopped. "What?"

Dad lowered his paper enough to look at Brad over the top. "You, um, you having a good time back home so far?"

"Yeah." What was this? Since when had his dad started making chit-chat with anybody, least of all him?

Dad raised the newspaper up again and cleared his throat. "Good. That's good."

Brad paused at the open door for just a second, waiting to hear if his father would say anything else.

The only sound was his dad turning another page in his paper.

CHAPTER 40

Megan pulled up to the hospital entrance. "How long until you want me to come back?"

Scott unbuckled. "Maybe an hour or so. You can drive Susannah home, and I'll stay with Kitty for the night. You know where you're going? Want me to show you how to use the GPS or anything?"

"No, I'm fine." Did he think she used GPS to get herself around Costa Rica?

Scott paused before getting out of the car. "There's not much, but go ahead and look around town. Walmart's just up Main Street a little way, couple miles past the church. The Christian bookstore went out of business, or I'd send you there too."

"It's fine. I was thinking I'd find something for Susannah and the baby since I won't be here by the time she delivers. Is there anything you guys need for the nursery?"

Scott sighed. "You'd have to ask her. She's been collecting a few things at yard sales and stuff, but I really couldn't say what she's grabbed and what she hasn't."

"No problem. I'll just look around and see what I find."

"Well, don't worry about anything too fancy. You've seen how small the house is."

"All right. Say hi to Kitty, and let Susannah know I'll be praying for everyone. You have what you need?"

"Let me just grab my bag from the back seat, and I'll be set."

She said goodbye to her brother, looking forward to a little time alone. That was something she'd discovered about herself early on in Costa Rica. She could pour her heart and energy into her work, but she needed to carve out at least a little time every day to unwind, preferably without anyone else around.

She pulled out her phone to search for gift shops in the area. She refused to buy her new niece or nephew a present from Walmart if there were any other options. The problem was figuring out what stores would be open at eight o'clock on a Saturday night. There had to be something.

One of the gift shops listed had a cute website and stayed open late in the summer. If it wasn't too far, she could get there by closing. She tapped on Google Maps, pulled out of the parking lot, and rolled the windows down in her brother's car.

She was ready to enjoy a little peace and quiet.

CHAPTER 41

Baxter Loop looked a lot closer on Google Maps, but Megan eventually found her way onto a long dirt road. If it weren't for her little car emblem on the GPS screen, she would be certain she was lost. The gift shop should only be another few miles away.

Sure enough, before long she started passing signs for the Safe Anchorage Goat Farm. The gifts on their website looked really nice, and she was sure she could find something fitting for Susannah and the baby.

If she got to the store before it closed. She had to drive so slowly on this dirt and gravel she'd be cutting it pretty close.

Finally she pulled up in front of a large farm house. Off to the right was a building with a sign that said *Gift Shop*. The open light was still on in the window. Good.

She parked the car and got out. She should have asked her brother what kind of things Susannah liked for herself. Oh, well. If the gift shop was half as nice as their website, it wouldn't be hard to find something appropriate.

The doors jingled when she entered.

"Hello, there." A plump woman, slightly past middle age, stepped out from behind the counter, wiping her hands on a red checkered apron. "Welcome to Safe Anchorage. Are you looking for anything in particular?"

"Not really." Megan was much more of a browser. She glanced up and down the artistically displayed lotions, soaps, and candles.

The woman smiled. "Well, you take all the time you need. My name's Connie, by the way. Just give a shout if I can help you with anything. Are you looking for something for yourself or a friend?"

"A friend. My sister-in-law's pregnant."

Connie bustled down an aisle. "Well, we've got all kinds of choices. Are you shopping for the baby or the mama? If it's for the little one, we've got some unscented lotions, very healthy for that soft newborn skin. If it's something for the mama, it really just depends on what she'd like. We've got candles and lotions and jewelry ..."

Megan could get lost in these aisles. "I'll just look around for a little bit. Thanks."

Connie busied herself straightening some colorful scarves on their hangers. "Are you from out of town?" she asked. "I don't think I've had the pleasure of seeing you here before."

"Yeah, I'm just visiting for the summer."

"Where are you from?"

"The East Coast originally, but I've spent the past few years in Costa Rica."

"Really? What is it you do there?"

Megan thought about what her brother had said earlier, about how it had been hard for him giving up his title when he married Susannah and settled down in Orchard Grove. "I'm a missionary."

Connie's smile widened. "That's wonderful, dear. We need more people ready to lay down their lives for the Lord."

The bells on the door jingled. "Mom, I need some help with Peaches. I can't get her into the ..."

He stopped.

Megan turned around. She was staring at Brad.

"Oh." He was just a few feet away. She could reach out and shake his hand if she wanted.

"I was just making a new friend." Connie bustled forward. "This is my son Brad, and I'm afraid, honey, I didn't think to ask your name."

"I'm Megan," she managed to stammer even though her voice was hardly above a whisper, "but your son and I have already met."

CHAPTER 42

Brad couldn't believe it. Out of all the random customers who could stop by the gift shop this late at night …

"You said Peaches is giving you a hard time?" Mom asked.

"Yeah." That pink goat of hers would drive him insane. He'd never met a more stubborn, ornery animal.

Mom smoothed down her apron, "Well, now, I'll go check on her if you don't mind closing up."

For a minute, he thought his mom was intentionally leaving him in here alone with Megan, but as she hurried out the door calling to her favorite goat, he figured she was probably more concerned about Peaches than anything else.

He stood staring at Megan.

"Hey."

"Hey."

What was supposed to happen now?

"How's your grandma?"

"What?" For a minute, he'd forgotten that she'd seen him

at the hospital. "Oh, Grandma Lucy? She's all right. She hit her head and needed a few stitches. Nothing too serious."

"That's good."

He glanced around the store, hardly able to think straight. "Want to sit down?" he finally asked. "There's some chairs in the back."

"I'm just doing a little shopping. I won't be long."

"Oh."

"Susannah's sister's sick."

"Really? That's too bad. Is that what you were doing at County?"

She glanced at the floor. "Yeah."

It certainly wasn't the way he had hoped for their first real conversation to go. "I came back to see if you were there in the waiting room. After they got Grandma Lucy situated. You'd already left."

"Oh."

He cleared his throat. Why did this have to be so awkward? When in Vermont had they ever run out of things to say? He thought back to their last night together, staying up while the stars twinkled overhead. Did she remember any of that? What about that shooting star?

The memory gave him an idea. "Hey, how big of a rush are you in?"

She looked as uneasy as he felt. "I've got a little bit of free time. Why?"

He switched off the open sign and locked the door. "Come with me. There's something I want to show you."

CHAPTER 43

"Last time we went star-watching it was a lot colder than this." Brad winced. Why had he said that? Was he just trying to bring up painful memories?

"That was a good night."

Heat seared through his body at her words. Did she remember their parting kiss?

He cleared his throat. "I used to come out here all the time when I was a little kid. Thought I could count them all if I was just out here long enough."

She leaned back on the roof. "It's lovely."

He glanced over at her, wondering what she was thinking. They'd hardly said a word since they got up here.

He let out a little cough. "Tell me a little bit about Costa Rica. Is the school doing well?"

"Mm-hmm."

They were going to have to find more to talk about or this would turn into the most painfully awkward and prolonged few minutes of his life.

"Is it hard to be away, or is it nice to have a little bit of a break?"

"Both."

He could understand that at least. That's exactly how he felt about being back in Orchard Grove.

She turned toward him slightly. "What about you? How are things at the boys' home?"

"Good." Come on. He needed to find something they could talk about, something that wasn't a landmine of painful memories or hurt feelings.

"How's Susannah's sister? Do the doctors think she'll be okay?"

"It's hard to know. Last I heard, there was at least a little bit of talk about sending her to Seattle. I guess it's kind of serious."

He glanced down at her. She looked so tender, so innocent. She cupped her hands behind her head and stared up at the sky. If she had any memory at all of their last night together, she wouldn't appear so comfortable.

He pulled out his phone and made a show of checking the time. "When did you say you had to be back to County?"

She sat up. "Pretty soon. I should probably go."

He stretched out his arm but stopped before touching her. "Careful. Watch your balance."

"I'll be okay."

She reached out for the branch they'd used to climb up here.

"Can I give you a hand?" he asked.

"No. I'll make it."

This was all wrong. *God,* he prayed, *if something else is supposed to happen here, please show me what to do.*

Or maybe this was exactly what the Lord had in mind. One last chance for Brad to realize nothing was ever meant to pass between him and Megan besides what already had. And maybe even that much had been a mistake.

Especially their kiss …

He started after her, and she paused with her feet on a branch. Stared straight at him with a look that shot hope and longing and despair surging through his heart at once.

"You okay?" he asked.

She turned away. The moment was gone. "Yeah, I'm fine."

She climbed down the tree and landed on the grass below without a sound.

CHAPTER 44

Megan had never felt more confused in her life. It wasn't like she had sought Brad out. It wasn't like she knew she'd run into him when she came to buy her sister-in-law a present at the gift shop.

He'd seemed happy to see her. Eager to show her the view from the rooftop. But once they got up there, everything had turned so painfully awkward. Her whole body shivered even though there wasn't the slightest hint of a breeze.

They were silent while he walked her to her brother's car. "You need anything before you go?" he asked.

Megan still hadn't bought a gift for Susannah, but it was too late for that now. It was a mistake coming here in the first place. Why hadn't God warned her this would happen if she came to Orchard Grove?

She paused by the car door. Surely there had to be more than this.

But what?

She turned around. She would tell him. It was as simple as that. Tell him how hurt she'd been when he moved on without sparing her a second thought. Not to make him feel bad. Not to pass judgment. Just to get it out there in the open.

She licked her lips. "Thanks for sharing your roof."

No, that's not what she intended to say.

He shifted his weight from one foot to the other. Again, she was vividly aware of how close he was standing. Her body still remembered being wrapped up in his arms, how secure, how loved, how cherished she had felt.

But that was all in the past.

Why even bring it up?

She shouldn't.

She opened the car door.

He cleared his throat. Was he about to speak?

He leaned forward, and her pulse raced.

"Well, drive safely."

She let out an exhale. She could finally breathe again.

"Yeah. Nice running into you. Thanks again for the view."

CHAPTER 45

Brad winced when Megan slammed the car door shut. *Go after her, idiot*, his heart shouted, but his mind just replayed how stupid he'd felt after flying all the way to Costa Rica just to find out she'd completely forgotten about him.

It was supposed to be this huge surprise. He hadn't told her he switched his plane ticket. For one thing, she would have balked when she found out how much he had to pay. For another, they'd both agreed that maybe the snowstorm was God's sign that they needed to take a step back. Slow things down a little. Pray more about their relationship.

Stupid how naïve he'd been.

And how much time and money he'd wasted flying out to surprise her.

He would never forget the shame that burned in his gut when he showed up at her school only to find her sitting in some courtyard, hugging another guy. At least at that point he'd possessed the decency to turn around and leave. What he really wanted to do was walk straight up to the stranger and punch him in the face.

But Megan had never been his to begin with. Sure, there was that kiss. There were those perfect nights together gazing up at the stars.

There were long, flowery emails. Late-night phone calls.

But none of it meant anything to her.

It was just as well she was gone.

Brad wasn't willing to make a fool of himself a second time.

CHAPTER 46

Breathe. She just had to remember how to breathe.

Megan's heartbeat was skipping around in her chest, and her fingers trembled when she tried to tell Google Maps to take her back to the hospital.

Stupid. Stupid of her to let herself get so carried away. Following Brad up the tree to the rooftop to look at the stars. How many other girls had he taken up for that exact same view? What about the worker who came to replace her in Vermont, not only at the girls' home but in Brad's arms too? How many times had the two of them bundled up in their snowsuits and counted shooting stars?

It wouldn't hurt so much if he'd told her the truth, but she found out about it online. Right after they were supposed to spend a perfect, blissful vacation together in Costa Rica, his online profile said he was dating the newest worker at the girls' home.

She shook her head, hating herself for even caring. Players like that weren't worth her emotional energy, but ever since she'd run into Brad at the bank earlier, she couldn't get him out of her mind.

God, I just want to move on. Can't you help me do that?

The problem was life was so busy in Costa Rica there was no time to think about dating. The only other single worker at the school was a sixty-five year-old widow, and their mission was isolated enough it was next to impossible to meet Christians besides the other Kingdom Builders missionaries. She'd tried long-distance dating once with Brad, and she certainly wasn't going to open herself up to heartache again by looking for a boyfriend online.

And what kind of boyfriend would she meet who wouldn't try to pull her away from her work? Her ministry?

Her calling?

So that was that. As long as she stayed in Costa Rica, she would remain single. And until God told her that her work there was through, what choice did she have?

She disagreed with her brother's assessment. She moved to the mission field to obey the Lord, not to run away from her past. Scott could talk all he wanted about the vain desire to be called a missionary or the convenience of living thousands of miles away from dysfunctional relatives, but if Megan wanted the easy life, she wouldn't have chosen Costa Rica. That much was certain.

And it's a good thing she left when she did, otherwise she might never have learned what Brad was really like. She shuddered to think of what might have happened if she'd stayed in Vermont, with their growing intimacy clouding out her better judgment.

Yes, God had spared her from making the biggest mistake of her life and getting even closer to Brad. Now that she knew what kind of person he really was, she just had to be careful that she didn't fall for him again.

There was no way she was willing to make that same mistake twice.

CHAPTER 47

Megan was late getting back to the hospital. Great. She parked her brother's car and hurried inside. After telling the woman at the front desk who she was, she headed down the hall to Kitty's room.

The doctor was there when Megan walked in. Scott was standing with his arm around his wife, and Susannah sat on the edge of her sister's bed. Megan glanced over. Kitty was asleep.

"Do you really think it's necessary?" Scott was asking. Megan could practically reach out and hold the tension in the room in her fist.

Janice adjusted her stethoscope. "If you want my professional opinion, I think Seattle's going to be the best place for her. If you're asking me as a friend ..."

"Yes, Susannah interrupted. "Yes, that's what we're asking."

Janice let out a sigh. She glanced at Kitty again and whispered, "Are you sure she's asleep?"

Susannah nodded.

Janice looked serious. "Your mom and I had several long discussions about Kitty's long-term health. And several times your mom considered signing a DNR form."

"DNR?" Scott asked.

"Do not resuscitate," Susannah answered without raising her eyes.

Now it was Scott's turn to sigh. "What did she finally choose?"

The doctor frowned. "She was still trying to make up her mind when she got in that car accident. So right now, I'm afraid the decision is entirely up to you."

Everyone stared at Susannah, including Megan, who felt vicariously burdened with the weight of that sort of responsibility.

"I don't know," Susannah whispered.

"You don't need to decide now," Janice assured her. "But if we can't help her here, and if they don't have any better answers in Seattle ..."

Scott squeezed his wife's shoulder. "What do you think we should do, babe?"

"Mom and I never really talked about this. I thought we'd have more time. I didn't think I'd have to make this kind of decision for years."

Scott forced a smile. "Hey, right now we're not talking about anything more serious than transferring her to Seattle sooner or later. That's the only decision we need to make right now, right, Doc?" It was just like him to try to make the best of a situation like this.

Janice nodded, and Megan felt herself breathing a little easier.

"Do you want me to call and make the arrangements for her transfer?" Janice asked.

"Why don't you give us a minute," Scott told her. "Let us talk about it and pray, and we'll let you know our answer soon."

CHAPTER 48

"So there you are, boy."

Brad stared down at his dad, who was standing below the climbing tree. He sighed. After Megan left, he'd worked his way back out here to give himself room to think. He should have known that even a few minutes' worth of privacy was too much to expect.

He slid off his star-gazing spot on the roof and started the climb down.

"Watch your step," his dad said as Brad hopped to the ground.

"What do you want?"

"Want?" His dad leaned over and spat on the grass. "I want to know who that gal was you had up on the roof with you earlier. And why you didn't invite her in like a nice, proper boy. And why you've been moping and avoiding me ever since you came home."

"I'm not avoiding you."

"Sure you are. I may not have any college degree like

you, and I may not have wasted all my best years preaching the gospel to hooligans and drop-outs, but I'm not an idiot. I know when someone's going out of their way to ignore me."

Couldn't this conversation wait a few decades or longer? "I'm just tired. It's been hard adjusting to the time change, and Grandma Lucy hasn't been feeling like herself ..."

"Well, you've got time for her. What about time for the man who raised you?"

He shrugged. What did his father expect? "I've got time for you right now. What do you want to do?"

"I could use a hand putting the new milk-stand together."

Why had he even asked? "Seriously? You want to do that right now? In the dark?"

"That's why we've got a light in the shed, you know. Nice little invention named electricity."

Brad thought he detected a glimmer of a smile that looked completely out of place on his father's face.

He sighed. "Fine. Let's go build a milk-stand."

A few minutes later, he was handing his father tools just like he had when he was eight years old.

"So you still never answered my question, boy."

"What question's that?"

"Who it was you had up on the roof. When I was your age, a boy didn't take a gal up to a secret spot like that unless they were up to no good or he at least was hoping to be."

"First of all, nobody really says *gal* anymore."

Dad spat onto the dirt floor of the shed. "Fine. What do you young folks call them these days? Should I say a chick?"

"No, that's even worse."

"Well, are you going to stand there lecturing me, or are you going to tell me who she is?"

"Her name's Megan. She's visiting her brother. He's the guy who married Susannah Peters earlier this year."

"Well, what's she doing on my roof, then?"

Couldn't his dad have picked any other night if he wanted help in the shed? And why did they have to talk about Megan of all people?

"She used to work at the girls' home in Vermont. We knew each other there."

"And?"

"And that's it."

"That still don't explain what she was doing on my roof."

Brad felt his blood pressure rise. "We were just talking, Dad, that's all. Is this some kind of inquisition? Do you want to hook me up to a lie detector or what?"

His dad took a step back, keeping his eyes on the wood. "It was a simple question, son. All I needed was a simple answer."

"Fine. We were talking. Is that simple enough?"

"Now, why you gotta be like that?" It was infuriating the way his dad couldn't even speak in a complete sentence. How was Brad supposed to stay out here for however long it took to make this milk-stand without losing his mind? Was it his mother? Was she the one who sent Dad out here so they could have some sort of bonding moment?

It didn't work like that. It was too late.

By a decade or more too late.

"I'm not being like anything," Brad mumbled. "You asked a question, and I answered it."

"Yeah, but what I'm wondering is why you got to give it with so much sass. I sure as anything taught you better than that."

Actually, you were so busy with your nose in the newspaper that you didn't teach me anything. Brad kept the thought to himself. Sometimes silence was better than speaking his mind.

His dad worked for a few minutes quietly. The job was simple enough Brad wondered why he even had to stick around. Dad certainly didn't need any help.

"So tell me something about this girl. You like her?"

"Not particularly."

"You thinking about dating her?"

"No."

His dad let out a grunt. "So what was it she did?"

"Huh? What do you mean?"

Dad straightened up. "She's pretty, she's single, and she's here in Orchard Grove where you don't gotta have an eagle's eye to notice there're not too many young gals around to date. She's a churchy one like you, she's here, so the only reason I can come up with why you don't want to go out with her is she did something to you in the past you're still stewing over like a broody hen."

Brad wished his dad would go back to working with his tools quietly.

"Well? What was it?" he pressed.

Brad let out his breath. "It's nothing."

"Good. Then it won't be no trouble telling me the whole story."

He wasn't going to let up, was he? "Fine." Brad huffed out the word. "We started talking in Vermont, I was going to meet her in Costa Rica ..."

"Whoa, whoa, whoa, back up. When did Costa Rica come into this story?"

Could his dad even follow a simple narrative? "She went to Costa Rica to become a missionary. I already told you that."

"No, you didn't. So she was headed off to be a

missionary in Costa Rica. Sounds like something right up your alley, Missionary Boy."

He hated when his dad called him that.

"So what was the problem?" his dad pressed, as if it were entirely that simple.

Brad gritted his teeth. "After she left for Costa Rica, I went to visit. It was supposed to be a surprise. But by the time I got there ..."

"She'd found someone else," Dad interrupted.

Brad stared at his father. "Will you let me finish my own story?"

"Sure. Go ahead."

Brad paused. What was left for him to say? "Yeah, she'd found someone else. How'd you know?"

Dad hitched up his jeans by the buckle. "Do I look like I was born in a barn?"

Brad figured it'd be best not to answer.

"So you got to Costa Rica, found you had a rival, and she picked the other guy instead of you. Is that it?"

"Basically."

"What do you mean 'basically'? That's either it or it's not. If she chose the other guy, well, there's not a whole lot you can do about it, but whatever choice she made back then, that's no reason to hold it against her now."

Brad felt himself deflate. "She never knew I came to visit."

"Come again now?"

"She never knew."

"And why in the name of Sam Franklin not?"

"Because I didn't tell her I was there."

"You an idiot or something?"

Brad couldn't tell if his father was making a joke. "No. But she'd obviously gotten cozy with this other guy ..."

"Wait, wait, wait." How did his dad ever expect him to finish this story if he kept interrupting like that? "Back up a minute. You actually saw them together? Do you mean *together* together? Or just together? 'Cause that's a big difference, you know."

"Just together. Do you want to hear what happened or not?"

"I'm listening, but right now what I'm hearing is a bunch of whining and complaining about some girl getting herself involved with another guy and you not even having the guts to let this little lady choose for herself who she wanted to end up with. Is that how it happened? You saw her with someone else and just packed your bags and left?"

"Basically." Except Brad didn't have to bother packing his bags since he wasn't at the mission long enough to unpack them to begin with.

His dad let out a chuckle.

"What's so funny?" Brad couldn't pinpoint a single part of the entire story that was remotely amusing. "Why are you laughing?"

"Because you're a fool. Sitting around moping like a crybaby because she chose somebody else when she didn't even know you were there. Of course she'd end up with that other guy if she never even knew you were interested to begin with."

"She knew," Brad mumbled.

"How? Did you tell her?"

"Not exactly. At least, not in so many words."

His dad bent over and slapped his leg.

"Would you cut that out?"

"Why? This is the most fun I've had since the dentist put me on that fancy laughing gas. You really aren't a bright one, are you? Listen, I know you and me have our differences, kid. You're probably still sore because I made fun of you when you went off to become a missionary and all that nonsense. That's water under the bridge now. 'Cause we're family, and yeah, sometimes we're gonna do things that drive the other mad, but you're still my son."

He shook his head, continuing to chuckle.

"So this gal, you just up and let her walk into someone else's arms far as I see it, and now you're stiff and sore with your feelings hurt. But I don't see her hanging all over someone else right now, do you? And if that's the case, then you're an even bigger fool to let her get away a second time. Anyway, that's just my two cents. Take it or leave it. But hand me that measuring tape, will you, boy? Hey, we're not done building this here milk-stand. Where do you think you're running off to?"

"Sorry, Dad. Love to stay and help, but I gotta go." Brad dashed out of the shed, ran into the house, and nearly plowed into his mother, who was dusting the china in the living room.

"Mom, Mom," he called out.

"Goodness," she gasped, "you nearly gave me a heart attack."

"Sorry, but listen, I need your help."

"What is it? You look awful. Are you all right?"

"Yeah, but can I borrow the truck?"

"Of course you can. But where are you off to so late?"

"Well, that's the other thing. I need to know where that girl you know lives. The one who married the missionary from the East Coast and now his sister is here visiting. Can you look up their address for me?"

CHAPTER 49

Scott let his wife lean against his chest, but Megan felt helpless and out of place. All she'd been able to do for the past ten minutes was hand Susannah more tissues.

"So we're telling the doctor to start the arrangements for Seattle, right?"

Susannah sniffed and nodded.

He kissed the top of her head. "I think it's for the best."

"I do too. I just … I don't know what we're going to do if things get any worse."

Scott held her close. "We'll worry about that when we need to, all right?"

Megan's heart was heavy. Who should have to make such terribly weighty decisions about their loved one's health? She'd heard about living wills and things like that before, but she'd always assumed they were important for old people her grandparents' age.

Scott stood up. "All right. I'll let Janice know. You gonna be okay if I leave for a few minutes?"

Susannah nodded. Megan handed her another Kleenex, but she'd turned around to look at her sister and didn't notice.

"What's that, sweetie?" Susannah leaned down toward Kitty. "I'm sorry. Was I being too loud? Did we wake you up with all our talking?"

Blink.

"How are you feeling?" Susannah ran her hand tenderly across Kitty's forehead. "I have some good news for you. Dr. Bell is going to make some phone calls to see if we can get you to Seattle. Remember the nice hospital there with the puppies that come to visit?"

Kick.

It was nice to see Kitty smile for a change.

Susannah took her sister's hand. "It's going to be great. Which puppy do you think will be there this time? The little tiny one with the short stubby legs?"

Kick. Kick.

"Or do you remember the poodle with the curly hair who gives you a handkerchief when you pretend to sneeze? *Ah-choo.*"

More kicks.

Susannah let out a musical laugh, and Megan felt the tension easing off her chest. Kitty was awake. She was happy and smiling. For the first time Megan had seen since they brought her to the hospital, she was responsive to the conversations going on around her.

All this talk about DNRs and everything else was just a formality. Kitty would be fine. There were specialists in Seattle who'd give her the care she needed, then she'd be back home in Orchard Grove in no time.

Megan was sure of it.

Any other alternative was too difficult to imagine.

CHAPTER 50

Brad's courage nearly failed him when he pulled into Susannah's and her new husband's driveway, but his body was surging with too much adrenaline to think of backing out now. There was nowhere to go from here but forward.

His conversation with his dad had been somewhat one-sided and certainly not the cathartic, heartfelt reunion they'd probably need if they wanted to improve their relationship permanently, but it had changed Brad's perspective. He'd often looked down at his father as a simple man, but that conversation in the barn had yanked Brad out of his pity-party and given him the courage to do what he should have done all the way back in Costa Rica.

He marched up the porch steps. He didn't care what time it was. She'd still be awake. She had to be.

He knocked on the door.

No answer.

He rang the bell.

Nothing.

Come on.

He glanced again at the address his mom had written on a flowery notepad in her slanted script. He was at the right place.

So where was everyone?

"Megan?" He pounded on the door. "Megan?"

He wasn't going to chicken out, not until he told her everything he should have said years ago. And then, just like his dad mentioned, it would be her choice what she did after that. But he wasn't going to let her walk away from him again without knowing the truth.

All of it.

"Megan? It's Brad. I want to talk to you."

Still no response.

Wait a minute. Hadn't she said something about the hospital? Susannah's sister was there.

He glanced at the empty driveway. Of course. She'd gone to County and still wasn't home yet.

It was just a few minutes' drive. He'd find her there. He had to.

He wasn't going to sleep tonight until she'd heard him out. Every single word.

CHAPTER 51

"I'll be back real soon, all right?" Susannah leaned over and kissed her sister on the forehead.

Megan stepped up to the hospital bed too even though she felt awkward talking to Kitty in such a cheerful voice when the situation was so serious. "I'm glad you'll be going to Seattle. Those therapy dogs sound really cute."

Kitty gave a tentative kick, which Megan hoped meant that she'd said the right thing.

Scott wrapped one arm around Megan and one around his wife. "You two need anything else?"

"No, we'll be fine," Megan answered. She and Susannah were about to run home and get packed for Seattle. It would take a while for Kitty's papers to come through and the transport crew to arrive.

"Well let me know if you need anything," Scott said. "I'll have my phone on."

Susannah kissed his cheek. "All right. Call or text if you think of anything else you want me to pack for you, okay?"

"Will do."

Megan and Susannah got to the car. A truck was speeding in right as they were pulling out.

"Wow," Susannah commented, "busy night at County."

"Yeah." Megan didn't know what else to say. She still needed time to process that awkward conversation with Brad on his rooftop, but all of that would have to wait while they worried about getting Kitty situated in Seattle.

"Are they transporting Kitty by herself or what?" she asked as she pulled onto Main Street.

"No, I'll probably ride along with her in the ambulance. And then you and Scott can drive out and meet us there tomorrow. I really don't want you on the road when it's so late and you're both so tired."

Megan was going to say that it certainly wouldn't be the first time she and her brother lost an entire night's sleep due to some sort of family catastrophe, but she kept her mouth shut.

"I'm glad you're here," Susannah confessed as they pulled into her neighborhood. "It's nice not having to worry about Kitty all by myself."

"I bet."

"My mom never mentioned the DNR." Susannah was speaking so quietly Megan had to roll up the car window to hear her. "Before she died," she continued. "I didn't know she was thinking about that."

Megan didn't know what to say. "Maybe she didn't want you to worry."

"I know. But I wish it was something we could have talked about. Now the decision's entirely up to me ..."

"Is it something you and Scott have discussed before?"

"Not really. I mean, Kitty's gotten sick once or twice since we got married, but it was never this serious, and it was never something where we thought ... I just didn't expect to have to have any discussions like this any time soon. Know what I mean?"

"I'm sure. What do you think your mom would have done?"

"From talking with Janice, it sounds like she was having a hard time making up her mind. Which is funny. If you'd known my mom, you'd know she was ready to go to battle for Kitty every single day of her life. I guess my first reaction would be to think that she'd never sign a form like that. No matter how bad things got. She'd feel like she was giving up on Kitty. But maybe ..."

Susannah didn't finish the sentence. Megan thought she understood what her sister-in-law was trying to say but didn't want to guess and end up being wrong.

They drove the rest of the way home in silence.

"Are you all right?" Megan asked as they walked up to the porch.

"Yeah. I'm just tired. And the baby's been moving around a lot. I don't think they like all this stress. Did you know your endorphins and stress hormones and things can travel through the placenta?"

"No. I didn't know that."

"I've been trying too hard to be calm and relaxed and happy, for the baby if for nothing else. But it's a lot harder than it sounds."

"I can believe that," Megan said. "Especially now."

Susannah sighed and took out her keys to unlock the front door.

"Right. Especially now."

CHAPTER 52

Brad ran into the ER entrance and stopped in front of the reception area. "I'm looking for a patient. Her last name is Peters. Why in the world couldn't he remember Susannah's sister's name? He wasn't thinking straight.

He stared at the woman, hoping she could read his mind. "The Peters girl?" he repeated. "She came in here earlier tonight. Can I go see her?"

The woman stuck a pencil behind her ear. "Visiting hours are over, I'm afraid."

"I'm not visiting, this is ..." He stopped. He couldn't technically call this an emergency, no matter how important it was in his mind. "Listen, it won't take me longer than a minute. I need to talk to her sister. Please. I don't even have to go in the room. If you could just let them know I'm here."

"You want me to tell them you're here?"

"Just find Megan. She's the one I'm looking for."

"And that's the patient's sister?"

"Yeah. I mean, wait. It's sort of like her sister-in-law. Or something like that. Just please tell Megan that Brad's here to see her."

The same nurse who had prayed with Grandma Lucy earlier that night hurried by, and the receptionist called her over. "That patient Kitty, the one with CP, can you let the family know there's someone who wants to see them?"

Ruby shook her head. "Last I heard they're getting the patient ready to transfer to Seattle, and the family went home to pack their things."

"They're home again?" Brad was already halfway to the exit.

"Do you want me to give them a message when they get back?" the receptionist called after him.

"No," he shouted. "I've got to run. Thanks!" A few minutes later, he was in his truck speeding back in the direction of Susannah's house.

He had to get there in time.

CHAPTER 53

"What else do you want me to pack for Scott?" Megan was thankful to have found a job she was qualified for.

Susannah tossed a few shirts into the open suitcase on the bed. "He likes to sleep in his flannel pajama pants. He usually just throws them under his pillow when he's not wearing them. You can look there."

Megan reached under the pillow. "I don't see any."

"You could check the lower shelf in the closet. There might be a clean pair there."

"I found them. Should I grab a sweatshirt or anything? Does it get cool in Seattle?"

"Not really. But he likes clean undershirts. They're in the drawer above the socks."

"Got them."

With as fast as they were packing, you might have thought they were trying to outrace a tornado or flash flood even though both Susannah and Scott had mentioned that the actual medevac process was painstakingly slow. It would probably be another hour or longer before Kitty was on the road.

"What about for fun? Should I find him some books or anything?"

"That's a good idea." Susannah tossed a flowered journal into the suitcase. "He's got a whole shelf full of missions books and biographies behind the loveseat in the living room. Just grab a few of those."

"Any particular titles?"

"No, he'll literally read anything on missions."

Megan made her way to the living room when she saw headlights shining in through the window. "Susannah?" she called down the hall. "Are you expecting anyone?"

"No." She came down the hall carrying pink satin pajamas. "It might be my stepdad, though. Janice may have told him what's going on. I wouldn't be surprised if he stopped by to see if there was anything we needed."

Someone knocked. Susannah opened the front door and exclaimed, "Oh. You're not Derek."

"No, I'm not."

Megan's heart stopped when she heard the familiar voice.

"Hi, Susannah. I'm sorry to hear about your sister. Mind if I step in? I really need to talk to Megan. Is she home with you?"

CHAPTER 54

Megan couldn't get over how dry her mouth was. She kept staring across the table at Brad. What was he doing here? Did he have any idea how busy they were?

"Listen," he began, "I know this is probably really bad timing."

His sense of understatement was almost comical. She needed to be helping Susannah pack. Not getting herself even more confused. If there was something he was dying to tell her, why couldn't he have mentioned it when they were alone together on the roof?

And how had he tracked her down here, anyway? Was Orchard Grove really that small a town that everyone knew where everyone else lived?

"I was thinking. We never really talked about what happened after you moved to Costa Rica."

No, not now. Did he seriously think she could handle a conversation like this when they were getting ready to rush Kitty to the Seattle hospital?

"That was a long time ago," she began. "It's really not worth rehashing."

"Well, I think it is, because there are some things you don't know."

Yeah right, she thought to herself. *Like how you started dating someone else from the girls' home when you were supposed to come visit me in Costa Rica. Or how you promised to come that summer when the snow kept you from making it for Christmas, but you just fell off the face of the earth and never wrote or called ...*

No, it definitely wasn't the time for this conversation.

She took in a deep breath, trying to find the right way to make him leave. She had to help Susannah pack for Seattle. They hadn't even made their way to Kitty's room yet. There was her favorite quilt and her *Adventures in Odyssey* recordings ...

Brad licked his lips and strummed his fingers on the table. "I know you're in a rush, but there's something I have to get off my chest. Then I'll be on my way."

So that explained it. He was still riddled with guilt all these years later, and he'd come here to apologize so he could sleep easy at night again. Well if all it took was Megan sitting here listening, she could give him a few minutes.

No more.

"What is it you want to tell me?" The faster they got through this conversation, the sooner she could go in the back room and help her sister-in-law pack.

"I flew out to Costa Rica to see you. After the snow cleared."

"You did?"

"Yeah. I did."

"Why didn't you tell me?"

"Because, stupid me, I thought you'd be happy to see me. I thought I'd make it a big, giant surprise."

"So what happened?" How could he have made plans like that without telling her? "What kept you from coming?

"I did come. I flew into San Jose, took the bus, made it all the way to the mission complex."

"I never saw you."

"That's because you were too busy with your new boyfriend, and I didn't want to make things even more awkward than they already were."

She stared at him. "What in the world are you talking about?"

"Your boyfriend. You were right there in the open, and I saw you. He got out of a cab, you ran straight into his arms, gave him like a dozen kisses. He swung you around in the air ..." Brad shook his head. "I didn't think that after everything we'd gone through together in Vermont you'd move on that quickly."

"Wait a minute. You saw me with someone else?"

There was an edge in his tone now. "Yes, I saw you. Were you just listening to me? After I paid double my ticket price and changed all of my holiday plans because I was so excited to see you, and I'd even gotten you this … well that's irrelevant now. But yes, I saw you there, and so I went away, and I guess I'm here because … because … Well, after I went through all that trouble to be with you, I hate to put it this way, but I feel like you owe me an explanation."

Megan wondered if her ears had stopped functioning. She was the one who owed him an explanation?

This was like a joke. A really bad, terrible, not-even-close-to-being-funny joke. "You should have told me you were there."

He shrugged. "What would it have changed?"

There was nothing more unattractive in a man than self-pity. "It would have changed everything." She heard the impatience in her own voice but didn't care. Who did he think he was, demanding an explanation from her? "That man you saw me with, the one who got out of the cab and hugged me? That was my brother, Scott. That's who I'm in town visiting right now."

He stared at her and blinked. "What?"

"That's my brother," she repeated. "He came out to see me because I was so lonely spending my first Christmas on the mission field by myself, and I was so hurt because you ..." She sniffed. Great. Was she seriously going to start crying now, after all these years? He wasn't even worth her tears.

"You moved on and started dating someone else, and I was having a really hard time accepting it."

He leaned forward. "What?" He looked as incredulous as she had felt a few minutes earlier.

"I'm talking about the girl who came to replace me at the girls' home."

"Rachel?"

"I don't remember her name. It doesn't matter anymore. But it was the same week you had planned to come visit me in Costa Rica when you were up there on social media posting about how you'd finally found the girl of your dreams and how happy and excited you were to be together."

She wiped her cheeks angrily.

"I have no idea what you're talking about."

She blinked at him through blurry eyes, wondering if he could have actually forgotten.

"You seriously don't remember?"

"Remember what? Megan, there was never another girl."

"You posted that you were super excited because you'd found the woman of your dreams and you couldn't wait to spend Christmas with her."

"I wrote that about you. That was before the snowstorm came. That was when I still thought I was going visit you in Costa Rica."

"Well, I sort of thought so too, or at least I was vain enough to hope that's what you meant. But then you got a new relationship status post, and it said you were dating that Rachel girl or whatever her name was. You never even told me."

He still didn't respond. Was he seriously going to deny it now when she had the evidence to support it all? She could go pull it up online if he tried to lie and say it never happened.

"Megan, that was a stupid practical joke."

Her pulse, which had been accelerating to the point where she could hear each individual thud, screeched to a halt in her chest. "A joke?"

"Yeah. Two of the teens at the boys' home got a hold of my laptop and wrote that as a stupid, juvenile prank. I posted that it wasn't true as soon as I found out what they'd done. Didn't you see that?"

She shook her head. Was now the best time to admit that she'd been so hurt at the news she'd blocked him?

He looked at her imploringly. "You seriously thought I was dating Rachel? After all we'd been through by then?"

"I didn't know what else to believe."

"Well, you could have asked me." Was he accusing her? Brad, the same one who flew all the way to Costa Rica just to turn around and go home because he saw her giving her brother a hug? Her brother she hadn't seen in years?

"So ..." he began tentatively, "this whole thing, then, is just one big misunderstanding?"

Yeah, he'd definitely perfected the art of understatement.

She stared at the table. "Sounds like it."

He let out a little chuckle. Try as she might, she couldn't see what was so funny.

"So that was your brother?"

"Yes." How many times would he make her repeat the same humiliating story, relive the pain and disappointment over and over again? "That was my brother."

He reached out, but she clenched her fist before he could take her hand.

"Listen, I'm so sorry. If I had known, I would have told you. I would have explained everything."

She didn't meet his gaze. "I really wish you would have."

He placed his palm on top of her fist. She blinked up at him. "Can we start over?" he asked. "I came here to ask if you thought it was too late."

She looked at his earnest face, remembered the fire that had surged through her the night of their one and only kiss. Thought back to how heartbroken she'd been that Christmas, thinking he had moved on so quickly.

But he had suffered too. Trite as it sounded, the whole thing really was one big misunderstanding, a misunderstanding that had caused so much disappointment.

And now he wanted to know if it was too late?

She didn't know how to answer.

She didn't have time to think about it. Susannah hurried out of the bedroom, her cellphone in hand. "Kitty's having some kind of incident. She's stopped breathing. We've got to go now."

CHAPTER 55

Brad didn't know what he was supposed to do. Megan jumped up from the table and threw on her shoes.

"Should I come too?" he asked. "Is there anything I can do to help?"

"I don't know," Megan called after as she followed Susannah out the door. "Just lock up or something, and I'll find a way to get in touch with you soon."

She slammed the door shut, and just a few seconds later he heard the sound of the car squealing out of the driveway.

What was going on? He had to get to County. He knew that much at least. There might not be a single thing he could do to help, but he wasn't just going to sit around at home, waiting to hear what had happened.

A few minutes later, he pulled in front of the hospital. He raced into the lobby, but he was the only one there.

"Can you tell me what's happening in the back?" he asked the receptionist.

She shook her head. "I'm sorry, I can't give that

information out to anyone but family."

Grandma Lucy's newest convert was hurrying by in her Garfield scrubs. "Ruby," Brad called out. "Hey, Ruby, can you tell me what's going on with Kitty?"

She looked at him and shook her head and hurried down the hallway.

Great. No answers. Well, what would you expect? Maybe he was stupid to have followed Megan here, but he wasn't about to leave when there was a chance that she might need him.

His cell phone rang, and he pulled it out. "Hello?"

His mom's voice on the other line was breathless. "Where have you been, honey?"

"It's a really long story. I can tell you when I get home, but it might be a while. Is everything okay?"

His mom sniffed. "Well, it's Grandma Lucy."

Oh no. This night was already too full of drama. He reached into his pocket, ready to pull out his keys and head back to the house. "How bad is it? I can be there in a few minutes."

Mom let out a coughing noise that might have been a chuckle or a sob. "No, it's not that. She's back to herself again."

"What do you mean? I thought she was doing well when

she came home from the hospital earlier."

"She was, but this is different. She woke up not long after you and Dad started working in the shed, and she's been in her prayer room ever since."

Brad failed to see how the revelation made much difference one way or the other. "She loves her prayer room. You know that."

"Listen to me." His mom spoke as if he were a little boy being punished for not paying attention. "She walked all the way from her room down the hall to the prayer room. She didn't use her walker or wheelchair or anything else. I didn't know. I would have never let her go that far by herself, but when I went in to see her, she was on her knees." Mom let out a stifled sob. "On her knees," she repeated, "just how she used to."

Brad still wasn't sure what all the excitement and the tears were about. "So she's had a good night. I'm just glad she didn't get hurt coming down the hall."

Mom still had that exasperated sound in her voice. "You'd have to see her to understand, I suppose. She's changed, Brad. She's different. You know how I've told you she's had her good days and bad days since her heart troubles last spring? This makes all of her good days seem like nothing. She's really herself again. I'm not one to go around saying this too readily, but I truly think it's some kind of miracle."

Brad mulled over the words. Grandma Lucy had certainly seemed invigorated earlier, especially after leading the nurse Ruby to Christ. But he hated the thought of getting his mom's hopes up too high only for her to be disappointed in the morning if Grandma Lucy woke up and didn't remember where she was or who she was talking to.

"Let's not get too carried away," he told her. It was a fine line between being sensible and reasonable and shattering his mother's faith. God certainly could have healed Grandma Lucy if he wanted to, but that didn't mean he had.

Brad waited for his mom to say something. "What's that sound?" he asked. "Is that one of the goats?"

"No." Mom was laughing. "That's Grandma Lucy praying. I can hear her all the way from the kitchen. Let me put you on speaker. You can listen for yourself."

Brad was about to tell his mom she didn't have to do that when the muffled noise in the background increased in volume, and he could hear Grandma Lucy's voice almost as clearly as if she were sitting in the seat next to him.

"You are the God of healing and power. You are the God who restores. You will raise her up from her bed of sickness and set on her head a crown of glory. For you are Jehovah

Rapha, the God who heals, the God who works miracles in our lives, unworthy as we are. It is your divine touch that will heal and restore her once again. For you, Lord, are mighty and you, Lord, will bring it to pass."

The powerful words again converted into muffled background noise, and then his mom was shouting excitedly in his ear, "See? She's better. She's herself again."

Brad had to admit that there was something different about the way Grandma Lucy was praying now compared to the other times since he'd been home. It reminded him of back when he was a child, and her prayer sessions over him were as constant and as regular as his mom's cinnamon rolls on Sunday morning or chocolate chip cookies after school.

Maybe God really had healed Grandma Lucy.

And if he could do that, who was to say he wouldn't perform that same kind of miracle for Susannah's sister as well?

CHAPTER 56

Megan held onto her brother's hand on her right and Susannah's on her left. Kitty's doctor joined the circle, as did the nurse in the Garfield scrubs who'd been taking care of her all evening.

"Father God," Scott prayed in a voice that rang out loud and clear, "we want to thank you for Kitty and for all the trials you've brought her through in the past, the healing that you've already shown her. Thank you, God, for the way that Janice and Ruby were able to respond so quickly when she stopped breathing. Thank you for the team from Seattle who's on the way to take her to the hospital there to give her the care she needs. Thank you for the grace that you've shown us tonight and for the fact that we can all be together right now.

"We confess, Lord, how scared we are for Kitty's health, how strongly we want to see her healed. We don't pretend to know your will, but we are certain that your arm is not too short to save. So if it's your will, I ask that you reach down and heal the infection that's in Kitty's lungs. Help her to get all the oxygen she needs and not have any more incidents like she just did. Help her to have a safe trip to Seattle, and whether she's awake or asleep or somewhere in between, Lord, I pray that your Spirit will keep her in perfect peace, that she wouldn't be in any sort of pain or fear. We love you, Lord, and lift this all up in the precious name of Jesus. Amen."

Megan let out the breath she'd been holding in. She and her coworkers prayed every morning before school started, but often their gatherings were little more than daily business meetings with a closing prayer tacked on at the end. She had no idea how God was going to answer their prayers on Kitty's behalf, but there was no doubt in her mind that their petition had been heard and had made an eternal difference.

She let go of Scott's hand and handed another tissue to Susannah who had started to cry during the prayer. "If you don't need me for the next few minutes," she told them, "I'm going to step out for a little bit. There's something I need to go check."

CHAPTER 57

Brad didn't even try to sit still. He'd been pacing the hospital lobby ever since he got off the phone with his mom. It was hard to say what he was thinking about more — Grandma Lucy, Susannah's sister, or Megan.

How stupid had he been? He'd never guessed that the man she'd been clinging to in Costa Rica might have been her brother. How many late nights had he and Megan stayed up in Vermont talking about this man she idolized — the one who shielded and protected her through the worst of the childhood abuse they suffered, her larger-than-life hero who was probably single-handedly responsible for Megan's wanting to enter the mission field in the first place?

The misunderstanding had been just as hard on her. To think that after one silly little online prank, she'd spent all these years thinking he had moved on to date somebody else. He didn't know if it was more funny or tragic. All he knew was that he would give just about anything to keep her from walking out of his life again.

"Brad?"

He jumped and turned around at the sound. He wanted to run to her, lift her off her feet and swing her around like her brother had that Christmas, but he stepped forward slowly.

"Any word on Kitty? I've been waiting to find out."

She nodded. "I thought you might be. That's why I came out here to check."

"Well, how is she?" He searched her face. Kitty couldn't be dead. God wouldn't let that happen, would he?

"They got her breathing again. But the infection's really bad in her lungs. There's a team from Seattle on their way to transport her there."

Brad wasn't sure what to say. "That's good news, isn't it? I mean, she'll get good care there, right?"

She nodded. She had grown even more beautiful over these past few years. Soft hair that he wanted to reach out and touch, skin so gentle he could almost imagine the velvety feel, and lips so perfectly kissable.

How could he ever forget those lips?

He took a single step forward. "So what happens now?"

"The Seattle team will be here before long. Then Susannah's going to ride with Kitty, and my brother and I are going to drive down in the car."

"That's not exactly what I was asking," he admitted.

She raised her eyes to his, and when he met her gaze, his whole body flooded with warmth. "I know."

"So we still have a little time before the Seattle team comes?" he asked.

She nodded.

"Is there anything you need to do back there? Anything you need to do to help get her ready?"

"No. We just finished praying, and now we're just waiting."

He gestured to a pair of seats in the corner. "Care for some company?"

Her chin quivered, but her smile spread softly across her face. "I'd like that. I'd like that very much."

CHAPTER 58

Time had never stood still like it did for Brad that night in the hospital lobby.

Knowing that at any moment Megan might be called away to Kitty's bedside made him hurry through everything he wanted to tell her.

And then some more.

According to the clock, they had been talking for a little over twenty minutes, but it felt like lifetimes.

"You're different," Megan finally admitted.

"I don't feel all that different." He grinned. "Unless you're talking about the fact that now I know how stupid I was to leave you there in Costa Rica."

She laughed. They had agreed to leave all their misplaced hurts in the past. Once the truth came out for them both, it was easy to do.

"So how am I different?" He wasn't sure he wanted to know the answer.

She was sitting so close to him. "You're older, for one

thing."

He laughed. "I guess that's what happens after nearly five years."

She shook her head. "No, I'm being serious. Not just your age. More mature, I guess."

"Not like the kind of idiot who would fly all the way down to Costa Rica to see you and then just head home like a puppy with its tail between its legs?"

"Will you stop talking about that? By the way, did those guys at the boys' home ever get in trouble? For changing your profile status?"

He sighed. "It was so long ago I don't remember. I'd forgotten it even happened until you told me how upset you were. You know, I thought a lot of our problems back then were because you felt God had called you to Costa Rica. I thought that maybe you looked down on me because even though I was working at the boys' home, I wasn't a cross-cultural missionary like you were. I didn't have to go out and raise my own support or get my passport stamped or anything like that."

"That's silly. We were both involved in ministry."

"I know, but there's kind of this hierarchy in Christian circles. Like there's the people who just go to church and work regular jobs. Then there's people like me doing full-time ministry but it's here in the States. Then there's the so-called *real* missionaries who raise their support and fly to other countries ... Do you get what I'm saying?"

Megan thought back to her conversation with her brother. "The way I see it, we've both been doing what God called us to do."

"So you never thought less of me for staying in Vermont?"

"What? No, of course not."

He let out his breath. "That's good. I thought maybe that was one of the reasons you were with that other guy. Like maybe I wasn't committed enough to the Lord to be worth your time."

"That's ridiculous."

He shared her laugh, even though this entire conversation was more tragic than comical.

She shook her head. "You know, I thought for months that you were dating Rachel because you thought she was a better believer than I was."

"Seriously? Are we talking about the same Rachel?"

"Yeah. I hardly got to know her, but she was the kind of Christian who's always wearing long skirts and grows her hair out and never raises her voice and comes from a family of like eight or ten kids. And when I thought you were dating

her, I figured you thought I wasn't feminine enough for you.
I mean, you have to have a certain amount of tomboy in you
to live where I've lived and do the kind of work I've done."

He grabbed her hand.

"No, don't say that." His voice sounded almost pained.
"That adventurous spirit, your willingness to just jump and
go wherever God tells you to go, that's what I loved about
you."

He stared at their hands and pulled away, clearing his
throat. "I'm sorry," he stammered. "I didn't mean ..."

A grin spread across her face. "What exactly didn't you
mean?"

She was really going to do this, wasn't she? Going to
make him spell it right out.

"Never mind."

If he stared at his lap long enough and if he was fortunate,
maybe she'd back down.

"No, tell me." No such luck for him tonight. "What was
it you didn't mean?"

"You really want me to say it?" He couldn't keep from
smiling when he saw the mischief dancing in her eyes.

"Yes. I really want you to say it."

He let out his breath. Yet again, she'd gotten the best of
him. "Fine. Back when we were in Vermont, and when you

left for Costa Rica, I thought I was falling in love with you."

There. Is that what she wanted to hear?

The grin was gone. So were the twinkling eyes. Had he said something wrong?

She glanced down at her hand. Why had he grabbed her like that? Didn't he have any respect for personal space?

"What about now?" she asked quietly.

His heart was pounding in his ears. "What do you mean?" he replied to buy himself more time. He needed to think through what he was going to say.

She shook her head. "Never mind." She smiled softly, but it wasn't the teasing grin he'd seen just moments earlier. "So tell me about how things are going at the boys' home. Is anybody still there from when I was around?"

He blinked. "Are you trying to change the subject?"

He watched the color drain from her face. "Yeah, but that's just because ..." She stopped.

"Because what?"

"Because it was wrong for me to put you on the spot like that. You know I was just having fun."

Having fun. Was that all this was? Maybe to her, but for him it was far more serious.

"You wanted to know how I still felt about you."

"Yeah, but I was mostly joking ..."

He shook his head. If he couldn't find his courage now, there was no guarantee he'd get this chance again. "You wanted me to say if I was still in love with you."

"I know. I'm sorry. I shouldn't have pushed it."

Would she let him speak his mind already?

"Do you want to know the answer or not?"

"Are you offering?" She raised her eyes to his. Hopeful.

"Yeah. Ask me again."

"What?" No wonder she was confused. So was he.

"Ask me again," he repeated, almost begging this time. He couldn't lose his momentum. Couldn't let his courage desert him.

"Ask you what?"

"You know." He was willing to make a fool of himself. The least she could do was give him a small push in the right direction.

She stared at him. "Are you sure this is the right time? The people from Seattle are going to be here soon to transport Kitty …"

"That's why I want to do this now." He'd let her walk completely out of his life before. He'd be a fool to repeat the same mistake again.

She let out her breath. "All right. What do you want me to ask you?"

"You know."

"No, I don't."

He sighed. Why was this so hard?

"If you have something to tell me," she said quietly, "just do it. We've known each other long enough. You can tell me anything."

She sounded so earnest. Through a small window, he saw her brother walking down the hall toward the lobby. It had to be now.

"All right." He'd already embarrassed himself tonight. Why not go ahead and finish the job? "You heard me tell you that when we were in Vermont, I thought I was falling in love with you."

She blinked at him, her eyes full of patient hope. "Yes."

"And then you started to ask how I feel about you now."

"Yes?" She leaned toward him.

His heart was thudding near his Adam's apple. He was certain she could hear it.

"And I've been thinking about it, and I think what I'm trying to tell you is ..."

Her brother burst through the doors of the lobby.

"The Seattle team is here," he told Megan without even glancing at Brad. "It's time to go."

CHAPTER 59

"You're quiet," Scott said as they pulled onto the highway on the way out of Orchard Grove.

"Yeah, just tired."

He sighed. "Well, it's late. It'll probably be three or four in the morning by the time we get to Seattle. You should try to take a nap or something."

Her brother was right, but how did he expect her to sleep at a time like this? Her thoughts swarmed around in her mind so chaotically she thought she'd get motion sickness even though she'd been riding those bumpy Costa Rican buses for years without a problem.

"Do you think Kitty's going to be okay?" she asked. Anything to get her mind off the conversation she never finished with Brad. When the two of them first sat down in the lobby, she thought they'd have to start over entirely. She'd been wrong.

But what was it he'd been about to say?

Scott turned on his windshield wipers. A slight rain was

falling. "God's pulled her through other sicknesses like this. We'll just have to hope and pray."

She wanted to ask what his opinion was about the DNR. She wanted to ask what he and Susannah would do if the doctors in Seattle couldn't find an antibiotic that could clear out the infection in Kitty's lungs.

But she was too tired.

The night was so dark.

And it would be a long ride to Seattle.

CHAPTER 60

Megan sat with her head in her hands, resting her elbows on the cafeteria table. She wondered how Scott and Susannah could stand the stress of Kitty's hospital stay without turning into horrible, irritable people. By their third day at the Seattle hospital, Megan found herself in such a surly mood she came here to the cafeteria so she wouldn't end up lashing out at anyone.

Kitty's condition hadn't worsened. That was the one blessing, but any improvements were progressing at about the rate of a snail inching its way along a garden gate.

It wasn't right. Scott and Susannah were both so loving, tender, and close to the Lord. All they wanted was to serve him with their lives. It wasn't fair for them to have such a tremendous burden. Not that Kitty herself was the problem, but their anxiety over her health was going to tear them apart. How could any brand-new marriage survive that kind of strain?

And what would happen when it came time for Susannah

to have her baby? Were they just going to come out here to Seattle every few months when Kitty got sick, exposing a newborn to each germ and pathogen in this hospital complex?

She really needed some coffee, but she'd left her wallet back in Kitty's room. That's how quickly she'd fled. Scott and Susannah were so focused on Kitty, so stuck in survival mode, they didn't even recognize how difficult a situation they were in.

It was the first time Megan saw her brother suffering and felt so powerless to step in and help. After all he'd done for her when they were growing up, she had absolutely no way to repay him.

She stood watching one of the hospital workers wiping down the tables. He walked with jerky movements, and a soft-spoken woman was going behind him, offering gentle reminders.

"All right, Mo. See this napkin here someone left behind? What do you need to do with that?"

The man nodded his head. "I go throw it away." He spoke with a slight lisp and practically yelled out each word.

"That's right. And what should you do with your rag when you go to the trash can to throw it away?"

"I should leave it here so it doesn't get trash-can germs

on it."

"Very good, Mo."

Megan turned away to keep from staring and nearly jumped from surprise when her phone beeped.

She pulled it out to read the text.

Any news on Kitty?

She smiled. She and Brad had stayed in touch over the past few days, and even though they never resumed the awkward conversation that had been interrupted the night of Kitty's transfer to Seattle, she sensed a growing intimacy. He usually called for a short chat around lunch time, and they spent an hour or more talking after dinner, and thrown in there were short texts throughout the day.

She'd been trying to come up with a way to broach the subject of Costa Rica again, to apologize for the anger she'd harbored against him. There were no words to describe how wretched she felt when she realized she'd been angry at him over a stupid internet prank. If she had only known he'd come out to Costa Rica to be with her ...

Well, the past couldn't be changed. And maybe that was for the best. They'd been catching each other up on years' worth of life and ministry, and it sounded like God had been using Brad at the boys' home to do some amazing work. There was no way for Megan to look back over her service at the Costa Rica school and deny God had wanted her to be there either.

Maybe the entire misunderstanding was God's way of keeping them both where he wanted them to be, and now ...

Now what?

She typed Brad back a quick response, wishing she had more to report. Everything now was focused on keeping Kitty comfortable and monitored so they could tell which drugs may or may not be helping her lungs. In her non-medical layman's terms, Megan figured the doctor's only real goal here was to keep Kitty alive long enough to find the medicine to cure her.

No wonder progress felt so slow.

Scott and Susannah were models of patience. Scott had canceled all of his work obligations except for a few meetings he could log onto over the hospital's guest wi-fi. The rest of the time, he was there for his wife and sister-in-law. He had spent their entire childhood watching out for Megan. Now he had Susannah and Kitty to care for. Megan was surprised at the unexpected feelings of jealousy that popped up every so often. It was a juvenile reaction, and one she'd never admit to out loud.

"All right, Mo," the woman coaxed from a few tables over. "What do we need to do now that everything's been wiped?"

"We missed one." He pointed at Megan's table.

"No, there's someone sitting there."

"Why's she look so sad?"

The woman lowered her voice. "This is a hospital, Mo. Lots of people are sad at hospitals. Now, we've cleaned all the tables we can ..."

"I didn't get that one," he protested.

Megan tried to pretend that she wasn't listening. The woman led Mo away, leaving Megan to wonder why the exchange left her heart feeling so heavy and burdened.

How's Grandma Lucy? she asked Brad. She hated how nearly every conversation of theirs started and ended with a focus on Kitty here in Seattle. Brad had problems at home to worry about too. Yesterday, Megan and he had stayed up until nearly midnight in the hospital guest house talking on the phone about his father. The two men had gotten into a major blowout years ago when Brad decided to go into ministry at the boys' home instead of staying in Orchard Grove like his father wanted. From the sound of it, she wasn't sure if Brad and his father were now more interested in reconciling or murdering each other.

She was just glad for things to talk about that weren't centered around this depressing hospital.

She texted Brad for a little while longer then glanced at the time. The lunch rush would be arriving soon. So much for her need for privacy. Oh, well. She was here for Scott and Susannah. The two of them hardly ever left the hospital room, even though Kitty was so sedated from all the medicine she was only awake for minutes at a time. Maybe Megan could convince them to take a walk in the fresh air, and she could sit with Kitty for a change.

She stood up with a sigh. As she made her way to the elevators, Mo hurried to wipe the area where she'd been sitting just moments earlier.

CHAPTER 61

"Come on. Are you ready?"

Grandma Lucy stood in the hallway. She even appeared to be standing straighter than she had when Brad first came to Orchard Grove. It was like watching her age in reverse.

"I'm ready, young man, but I still don't see why we need to drive all the way out to Seattle just to have a doctor tell you what I've been saying all week. God has healed me, and in his grace he's restored me to perfect health. I haven't felt this strong in decades."

Brad believed that much to be true, but the last thing he needed was for Grandma Lucy to get too optimistic about her newfound vigor and push herself too hard. He stared at the small scar on her forehead where Ruby had taken the stitches out just the day before.

"Have you used the bathroom?" he asked. "It's a long drive."

Mom bustled in from the kitchen and handed Brad two overflowing baskets and an ice chest full of food. "Here you are. I packed you a picnic lunch. I thought maybe once you got to the North Cascades you might want to pull over and enjoy the view. Here are some snacks for the road, and you know how expensive those Seattle restaurants are, so you'll find some fried chicken down here which I thought you could have for dinner. Grandma Lucy doesn't need it heated up, and I hope you don't either. Now, I've already put a thermos of iced tea in the car. Is there anything else you think you need?"

Brad eyed the contents of the baskets. "What, no eggs or goat milk?"

"Milk doesn't agree with Grandma Lucy's stomach too well these days. And I'm sorry. I was thinking about eggs but those naughty hens have been hoarding them. I sure hope we get some chicks soon or they won't be worth the cost of their feed."

He smiled. "I was joking, Mom. This is plenty."

She let out her breath. "Oh, good. Here, Grandma Lucy, let me help you with your shoes." She knelt down and turned to Brad. "You really shouldn't let her do this on her own. She might fall."

"I wish the two of you would stop worrying over me. The only reason I'm agreeing to go see that doctor is so he'll tell you I'm perfectly fine. Maybe then I can get some peace and quiet around here." Grandma Lucy's eyes twinkled even though she tried to make her voice sound stern.

"Now," Mom breathed, "you drive carefully. You have plenty of time ..."

"They'll be fine," Dad muttered from behind his newspaper. "Just let the boy go. You know he's only driving all the way out there to see that gal of his."

Mom slapped her thigh. "Oh, that reminds me. I nearly forgot." She hurried into the kitchen and came back with an overflowing gift bag. "This is for Megan. You know, she never did end up finding a present at the shop when she came out last week."

"I reckon that has something to do with him taking her out on the roof instead of letting a paying customer spend her money in our shop." If Brad had known his father better he might have thought he saw him wink at Mom, who set the fancy gift bag on the table and pulled out the contents one by one. "Now, I put in a few candles, even though I'm pretty sure they won't allow them to be lit in those hospital rooms, but they'll at least add some color and cheer. And here's some lotion. I couldn't remember if Kitty has sensitive skin or not, so I decided to play it safe and just put in the unscented kind, but you know that hospital air is so dry. I'm sure this is going to help keep her more comfortable. You tell Susannah she can apply as much as she wants, up to four, five, even six times a day if she needs.

"Now, let's see. I didn't know what to put in for Scott, but I've never yet met a man who doesn't love my cinnamon rolls, so those are mostly for him, but of course he can share with the others if he wants to. And Megan, well, I hardly got the chance to meet her, but I picked out a pretty scarf and a bracelet to match. You know, I was going to throw in some earrings, but she was only in the store for a minute or two, so I don't even know if she's got pierced ears, and of course you couldn't expect that to be something a man would pay attention to. So these are the gifts."

Brad wondered how his mom could get through that whole recitation without losing her breath. He leaned over to kiss her cheek. "That's great. I'm sure everyone will be really thankful."

"You drive safe now, you hear? And tell Megan that she's invited over for dinner soon as she gets back to Orchard Grove. Heaven sakes. Do you think she's bored at the hospital? Should I find a few of my novels to let her borrow?"

"I don't think she gets into Amish romance as much as you do. It's fine." He didn't bother to mention that with all the goodies Mom packed, he and Grandma and Megan's whole family could survive at the hospital for a week.

"Well, here." Mom pulled a pack of cards out from the junk drawer in the kitchen. "You take these. That way she and her brother can play some cards while they wait for Kitty to recover. Or wait a minute. Do you think they're the kind of family that plays cards? I don't even know. Will they be offended?"

"I'm sure it's fine."

At the rate they were going, he and Grandma Lucy would never make it to their appointment with the neurologist.

He took Grandma Lucy's arm.

"I can make my way to the car, young man. I don't need any help."

"Just trying to be a gentleman," he told her, and he led her outside.

CHAPTER 62

It was hard to believe she'd been here for a full week. Naively, Megan had thought that Kitty's health would either improve or deteriorate. She wasn't expecting day after day with no change at all. Even Scott and Susannah seemed to be having a harder time the longer they waited in Seattle. Last night, the two of them got into a fight about whether or not Scott should return home to Orchard Grove.

Susannah didn't want him to miss out on another full week of work. He refused to leave her side, especially with her being pregnant.

"What if something happens to the baby?" he demanded.

"Then it's a good thing I'm here at a hospital, isn't it?"

Halfway into the following day, they still hadn't made up their minds. Megan tried to stay out of their way. She didn't want to add to their stress.

She was at her usual table in the hospital cafeteria, watching Mo clean up from the lunch crowd.

"You done with your napkin?" he asked when he got to

Megan's table.

She glanced at the piece of trash several chairs over. "That's not mine," she said. "You can take it."

"You don't need it?"

She glanced around, wondering where the woman was who usually helped him clean. "No, I don't need it."

"Are you sick?" he asked. "Is that how come you're at the hospital? Or are you visiting someone sick?"

"Just visiting."

He pouted. "They gonna get better?"

"I hope so."

"Me, too."

"Mo," a familiar voice called from around the corner. "Mo, you need to come here and see which silverware containers need to be refilled."

He gave her a smile. "I've got to go."

"All right."

"Hope she gets better."

She stared after him as he walked off, whistling softly to himself.

Megan went back to her brooding. At least this time she had a cup of coffee to focus on in addition to her worries.

The one good thing she had to look forward to was a quick visit with Brad this afternoon. He was driving out to

Seattle to take Grandma Lucy to some sort of memory clinic, and if everything went as planned, they could spend a few minutes together before he had to turn around and drive home.

She thought she'd be either nervous or excited about his visit, but she was slightly impatient, and that was it. She was tired of waiting, tired of living in this hospital, tired of worrying about Kitty and Susannah and her brother, tired of feeling like she was always in someone's way.

If it weren't for her daily phone calls with Brad, she'd risk losing her sanity altogether.

"All right, Grandma Lucy. Let's sit here for a little bit and rest. It's about half an hour until your appointment."

She turned at the sound of the familiar voice, thankful that her heart could feel something besides stress and anxiety and exhaustion.

"Well, look who it is." Brad smiled broadly and held out his arms. It felt so natural to hug him, like the last time they had done it was just yesterday instead of nearly five years ago.

"You're early," she said.

He nodded. "We got a head start. I wasn't expecting to see you until after the appointment."

She was about to ask what the chances were that they'd

run into each other randomly in a hospital this large, but she'd been reminded since coming to Orchard Grove there were no such things as coincidences.

Brad pulled out a chair for Grandma Lucy.

"How are you doing?" Megan asked her.

She smiled. "I'm just fine. I'm here to get my clean bill of health, and that's all."

"I'm glad you're so much better."

"That's what happens when the Lord touches you." Grandma Lucy spoke the words so factually. It sounded great, this idea of God's snapping his fingers and taking away all your ailments.

But how did that explain why Kitty was still here in Seattle with no real, visible signs of progress? Sure, she hadn't gotten worse, which was probably something Megan should thank God for. But if he could keep Kitty from getting even sicker, couldn't he cure her altogether?

"How was the drive?" she asked Brad, ready to get her mind off illness and hospitals.

"We had a great time, didn't we?"

Grandma Lucy was busy watching Mo mopping the floor and didn't answer.

Brad shrugged and smiled at Megan. "How are you holding up? Are you going stir-crazy yet?"

"A little." There was no use denying it.

"Well, I don't know how long our appointment's going to take, but if we're out in time, maybe we can go for a little drive or something. Get you out of this hospital, have a picnic. Mom packed a feast."

"That would be nice."

He met her smile and held her gaze.

"It's good to see you," he said.

"It's good to see you too."

Behind them, Mo was whistling loudly while Grandma Lucy swayed in time with his music.

CHAPTER 63

"So." Brad stared at Megan. How was it possible that she looked even more beautiful than he remembered? He knew she was stressed out. She'd told him so over their numerous phone calls over the past few days. It was one of the reasons he'd been in a hurry to get to Seattle, that and to take Grandma Lucy to the neurologist.

By the way she'd been acting lately, you would assume she was at the pinnacle of her mental capacity. So how did that explain the times last week when she didn't even know who he was?

Megan smiled at him. He could sense her unease. Why hadn't he thought this through? A hospital cafeteria with his ancient grandmother wasn't exactly the most conducive setting for the kind of heart-to-heart he wanted to have with her.

The kind of heart-to-heart they desperately needed.

There was so much he wanted to say. How stupid he felt for letting her walk out of his life. How determined he was not to repeat that same mistake twice.

How speechless and awed he was when he thought about the way God had led both of them to Orchard Grove to spend their summer furlough together. To rediscover one another.

To reclaim their lost love.

At first, when they started talking again, he'd been afraid he was moving too fast. He didn't want to say or do something that would scare her away. Years had passed since they had any significant contact with one another. They had changed.

Their relationship had changed.

So why did he feel like they'd been in love for years?

He didn't want to get ahead of himself, but he didn't want to sit around and waste time, either, which is all he felt like he was doing right now.

"Any updates on Kitty?"

Grandma Lucy stood up. "Excuse me, children. That man just looks so lonely I have to go talk to him." She headed toward a man in a white coat hunched over his food tray in a corner of the cafeteria.

"Does she do that kind of thing a lot?" Megan asked.

Brad smiled and rolled his eyes. "All the time."

At least they were alone now.

He reached for her hand, scared she might pull it away.

She didn't.

Their eyes met, and she smiled. He would do anything to keep her in his life again.

"I'm glad we have the chance to spend a little time together before the appointment." Why couldn't he think of anything more than stupid chit-chat?

"Me, too."

He wanted to reach across the table and tuck that stray strand of hair behind her ear, but he contented himself with holding her hand. Memories of their kiss in Vermont flooded his entire body.

"We haven't really had any time with just the two of us since we ran into each other, have we?" he asked.

"There was that night on the roof."

He shook his head. "Don't mention that. Please."

"Why not?"

He groaned. "I was so embarrassed. I couldn't get out more than two or three words the whole time."

She continued to smile at him, so gentle and warm. "It was fine. I thought it was really sweet."

"You're just saying that to make me feel better."

She let out a musical laugh. "Well, maybe." She was staring at Grandma Lucy again. "What's she doing?"

Brad turned around. She had one hand on her new

friend's forehead and raised the other toward heaven. "She's just praying for him. Does it all the time."

Megan didn't say anything. What was she thinking about?

Brad glanced at the clock hanging up by the staircase. Only a few more minutes before he had to take Grandma Lucy to her appointment.

"So, um, now that we're alone ..."

Megan tightened her grip on his hand.

He swallowed. He could do this. "I wanted to ask you about what you think ..." No, that wasn't the way to start. He tried again. "I thought it would be good to take a little time to talk about ..."

"Excuse me," a tall man with a rag interrupted. "Are you done eating? I need to wipe the table."

Brad glanced around. Out of all the other tables in the cafeteria, what was so special about this one?

Megan's eyes were full of sympathy. He couldn't keep his feelings to himself. He had to tell her the truth.

He turned to the worker. "Mind giving us a few more minutes, and you can clean up when we go?"

The man frowned, then a woman called him over to another part of the cafeteria.

Brad clasped Megan's hands in both of his. "I know we

don't have much time, but I need to tell you how much I …"

"Are you ready?" Grandma Lucy interrupted from behind.

He let out his breath and glanced at Megan.

"You need to go, don't you?" She smiled at him graciously. Even if he hadn't been able to tell her everything that was on his heart, he got the sense that she understood.

"Yeah," he replied. "Hopefully our appointment won't take too long. I'll text you when we're done, and we can make plans for the afternoon."

He realized he was still holding her hand and let go.

It was still early in the day. They'd have time to finish their conversation later.

All the time in the world.

CHAPTER 64

Megan's short visit with Brad hadn't cured her of her worry over Kitty, but she certainly felt more hopeful than she had earlier.

Maybe God had worked out all the details of her trip to Washington from the start. He knew that she and Brad would run into each other, that they could finally do something to try to fix all the mistakes and misunderstandings of their past.

She took the elevator up to Kitty's floor, humming under her breath.

It was the same tune she'd heard Mo whistling in the cafeteria.

There was a small chapel on the way to Kitty's room, not the main one used for services, just a small room where family members could find a little solace. She stepped in.

Thank you, God, for the chance to visit with Brad. I pray you'll give Grandma Lucy a good meeting with the doctor.

She tacked on a selfish prayer that the appointment

would go quickly so she and Brad could spend more time together before he had to make the drive all the way back to Orchard Grove.

Please guide and bless our relationship. Show us what it is that you want us to do now that we're connected again.

It was strange. Since they were back in touch now, she felt closer to him than she had back in Vermont the night of that kiss.

If this isn't your will, God, please show us now before we get any closer.

She knew that she was always supposed to pray for God's will to be done, not her own, but in her heart she hoped that God's will included her and Brad getting the chance to spend more time together.

Lots more time.

Peace washed over her, and she inhaled deeply. She'd have to come back to this little chapel sometimes when the hospital environment got her too stressed. It certainly beat the cafeteria.

She returned to Kitty's room but stopped at the door when she saw her brother's expression.

She felt the blood drain from her face, and she held onto the doorframe for support.

"What's wrong? What is it?" She hadn't been gone that

long. What could have happened?

She hurried to Kitty's bedside, glancing at the monitors. "Is she getting worse?"

Scott shook his head. "No, Kitty's doing fine. But there's something I need to tell you." He picked up the TV remote and pointed it at the screen. "It's not good news. You should probably sit down."

CHAPTER 65

"I don't understand." Brad wondered why doctors had to make things so complicated. What was so hard about answering a simple yes or no question? "Does she or doesn't she have dementia?"

"Well, it's a little more complex than that." The doctor sat on his little spinning stool and stared at his clipboard. "The screening test showed some conflicting information, not typical of what you'd see in dementia or Alzheimer's patients. Her long-term memory is fine, which doesn't mean a whole lot. I've seen patients in the last stages of dementia who can still recite their first phone number or rattle off the birthdates of all their siblings."

So what? How did any of this apply to Grandma Lucy?

"As far as short-term, she did pretty well on that part of her screening too. If all I had was this initial test, without any biographical information or health history, I'd guess the patient was at most a middle-aged woman and the epitome of perfect health."

"I told you," Grandma Lucy inserted. "I've been healed. The Lord Almighty gave me a sound mind once again."

The doctor sighed. "That's the part I don't like. Given her health history, given how bad you say things were just a few days ago and how quickly the symptoms appeared after her heart troubles, well, it certainly doesn't rule out a somewhat atypical presentation of dementia."

"What's that mean?"

"It means that while she is apparently having a good day today cognitively and otherwise, it's also possible that her brain is establishing for itself an entirely new baseline. Think of a pendulum if you will. Some days, she might be perfectly lucid, perfectly high-functioning. But then there's the chance of transient ischemic attacks, that's mini-strokes if you will, that may be impairing her cognition. An MRI would reveal more, but since she's refusing any further testing ..."

"I don't need you to poke and prod when the Holy Spirit's already told me that I'm healed," Grandma Lucy huffed. Brad wasn't sure if he should make apologies to the doctor or not.

"That's the other thing." The specialist lowered his voice. "If you hadn't assured me that she'd always been this way, this degree of religious fervor could also be indicative of some underlying neurological issue."

"You think she's crazy because she talks to God?" Now Brad was leaning more toward taking Grandma Lucy home and never coming to this quack again.

"That's not quite it, and I certainly mean no offense. I'm just saying that any major changes in personality or behavior or cognition are important to note at this age. What I'd like you to do is keep a record over the next few weeks. That will give us more of a baseline, if you will, and give us a range to measure the scope of any deterioration. Then I'd like you to bring her back to see me in a month for further testing."

Brad glanced over at Grandma Lucy. She certainly didn't look confused or unhealthy. Then again, what did he know about the brain? Those mini-strokes the doctor mentioned sounded serious. He didn't want to miss anything simply because she insisted she was fine.

He reached out his hand. "All right. Thank you, Doctor."

The neurologist nodded and left. Grandma Lucy let out a disgruntled snort. "Oh, that man."

Brad tried to hide his impatience. "Come on, Grandma Lucy. Let's get you out of here." He'd wished for more answers when he came to this appointment, but at least the drive gave him a chance to see Megan. He was looking forward to spending more time with her before he had to head home. Time to finally finish that conversation they'd started.

His phone rang.

"Son, did you hear? It's terrible. Does Megan know yet?" His mom was nearly sobbing while she told him the news.

When the call ended, Brad shoved his phone in his pocket.

"Come on, Grandma Lucy. We've got to hurry."

It took every ounce of patience he could muster not to leave her there and run the entire way to Kitty's hospital room.

CHAPTER 66

Megan stared at the television screen.

"It can't be real." She wiped the tears that streamed down her cheeks, trying to clench off her throat to keep her sob subdued.

Susannah reached out and squeezed her hand. "I'm so sorry."

Megan shook her head, watching the devastation unfold while the ticker on the lower part of the screen shot out stats like a mechanical, unfeeling robot.

6.8 earthquake shakes Costa Rica.

Coastal towns evacuated due to tsunami risk.

On the screen, a mother cried while she held her small baby, both of them covered in dust and blood.

"Those poor people," Susannah breathed.

Megan couldn't hold back her sob.

Scott sat down beside her and wrapped his arm around her shoulder. "It's going to be okay," he whispered.

"Is there anyone you can call?" Susannah asked. "Maybe

someone can tell you how bad things were at the school."

"I tried that already," Scott said. "I've got the Latin American field director on speed dial. He said the phone lines are down. He hasn't been able to get in touch with anybody on the inside."

Megan leaned against her brother's shoulder and shook against his chest.

The door to Kitty's room burst open. "Megan, I just heard. I'm so sorry. Are you okay? Have you heard from your friends yet?"

She could hardly focus on Brad's face through her tears as he knelt in front of her. He wrapped his arms around her, arms that were just as protective and loving as her brother's.

"I'm so sorry," he whispered again. "Tell me what we can do. How can we help?"

Megan hadn't even noticed Grandma Lucy in the room, but her voice was strong and confident as she answered, "We do what any faithful believer does in a situation like this. We pray."

CHAPTER 67

Brad tarried by the door of Kitty's hospital room while Megan said goodbye to her brother and sister-in-law. He wondered how to recapture that fleeting moment of peace he'd felt when everyone in the room was praying together.

"I'm so sorry I can't help more with Kitty," Megan said.

Susannah wrapped her arms around her. "Don't feel bad. We'll keep you posted on Kitty's recovery, and you keep us posted on how things are going on the field."

"I will. And you better make sure you give me plenty of notice before your baby shower so I can Skype in. Assuming we've got the internet up and running by then."

Susannah smiled. "I promise."

Megan turned to her brother. "I'm sorry I couldn't stay longer."

He sighed. "I still wish you'd wait a few days. It's going to be chaos down there."

"That's why I need to go. Thank you so much for helping make the arrangements."

"Yeah, well, what's the point of knowing relief missionaries all over the world if you can't get your kid sister a flight to Costa Rica when she needs it?"

She leaned against his chest. "Thanks for understanding."

Brad stood watching her hug her brother, reminding himself how stupid it was to be jealous.

"Are you ready?" Scott finally asked. "You need to hurry, or you'll miss that flight I worked so hard to get you on."

"I'm ready." She turned and smiled at Brad. "You sure this isn't going to take too much time out of your day?"

He glanced at Grandma Lucy, who was asleep on the oversized chair next to Kitty's bed. "I'm sure. She was ready for a nap anyway. Those tests must have tired her out."

"I'm so sorry. I didn't even ask how the appointment went."

"We can talk about that on the way to the airport. You all set to go?"

"Yeah, hold on just a sec." She walked up to Kitty's bed and picked up the hand of the sleeping girl. "Bye, Kitty. I'm glad I got to meet you, and I hope you feel better soon."

It took a few more minutes for her to give her brother and sister-in-law one last round of goodbyes, then Brad held open the door, and they walked out together into the hallway.

CHAPTER 68

It was stupid for her to be crying like this. The moment she'd heard about the Costa Rican earthquake, she'd prayed and asked God to help her find a way to get back home. Back to her mission and her calling and the children and coworkers she loved.

And he'd answered. Her brother was one of the most well-networked people she knew, and one of his best friends was the Latin American field director for Christian Relief Ministries. If she could find a way to get herself to Atlanta, CRM would fly her down with the rest of the team they'd activated to respond to the quake.

She'd be home by this time tomorrow.

"Are you all right?" Brad adjusted the strap of her carry-on.

Good thing she was already packed for this trip to Seattle. There was nothing left for her at Orchard Grove now. Nothing except ...

"I'm in the parking garage. We should take the sky

bridge. It'll save time."

It was funny the way God answered certain prayers. Hadn't she been hoping for the chance to spend some time alone with Brad?

This certainly wasn't how she'd expected God to answer. But she wouldn't dwell on that now. Fear and anxiety propelled her forward.

Forward to home.

They reached Brad's car, and he set her bags in the backseat. She'd finally stopped sobbing like an idiot, but she was still a mess.

Oh, well. She was with Brad now, but only for the twenty minutes it'd take him to drive her to the airport.

Some prayers God answered right away, and some prayers he didn't.

He sighed when he sat down next to her.

She felt like she had to say something to break the uncomfortable silence. "Thanks again for the ride."

"It's the least I could do. Seriously. I just wish there were more."

Before he pulled onto the road, his eyes locked with hers.

"I know what you mean." What more was there to say? She thought about the conversation they had started to have so many different times. The conversation that even now sat unspoken between them like a barbed wire fence. "Listen, I know we were going to have that talk about ..."

About what? About a relationship that apparently was never meant to progress past a few wonderful memories that were years old by now?

"It's okay. You have other things to worry about."

"I know, I just wish ..." Wish what? What else was there to say? She watched as trees and buildings whizzed by relentlessly. "I wish things had worked out differently back then. You know?"

"Yeah." His voice was quiet. Reflective. "I know."

She cleared her throat. "I hope Grandma Lucy's okay. What did the doctor have to say?"

While he drove, Brad filled her in about Grandma Lucy's health, about the questions that even now remained unanswered.

"Well, I hope she keeps on improving," Megan finally said.

They drove past a sign for the airport. Were they that close already?

Brad cleared his throat. What was he going to say? And was Megan ready for it?

"I'm glad you're going back to Costa Rica. It's pretty obvious that's where God wants you to be, isn't it?"

As soon as the words left his mouth, she knew that this was how all their half-finished conversations were going to end. How they'd been destined to end from the beginning. Even that first awful Christmas so many years ago, she'd realized that if she were going to follow God's call to the mission field, that meant making certain sacrifices in her personal life.

Sacrifices like Brad, no matter how deeply she cared for him.

No matter how desperately she might have hoped for another ending.

Time surged ahead cruelly. The minutes to the airport spited her by racing past with effortless, menacing speed.

He was at the curb.

Her bag was in her hand.

She stared at her feet.

"I guess this is goodbye." Even when he said the words, there was a hint of hopefulness in his voice.

A question.

If she responded the way she knew she was supposed to, she would never see him again. They would look back on these past few days as a strange fluke that brought them some amount of closure that would open the way for them both to be free to pursue other relationships, other callings, other futures.

If she responded the way she wanted to, she would never be able to get on that plane and return to the friends who needed her.

The family who needed her.

The choice was as easy to make as it was painfully unbearable.

She nodded slightly and forced herself to meet his eyes. He had to understand.

"Yeah." Even now, the memory of his kiss so many years ago surged through her gut like a flame. She forced her voice to be steady, forced her mind to think of all the work that lay ahead of her, and answered clearly, "I guess this is goodbye."

CHAPTER 69

Three and a half weeks later

"Señorita Megan, the worker at the school says he's looking for the …" The little boy frowned. "*¿Cómo se dice en inglés, cable de extensión?*"

"Oh, you mean the power cord."

"Yeah." His face lit up in a grin. "The power cord. Do you know where it is?"

She glanced around. It had been almost a month since Costa Rica was hit by the most devastating earthquake in its history. Thankfully, two out of the three buildings in their mission complex still stood, but the village itself was a disaster zone. The only electricity they could get came from a generator, and half the homes had been destroyed. The promised government aid had stalled multiple times, and practically everyone within ten miles was depending on the mission for their basic necessities.

Megan was so busy keeping the young families in the

area from starving, rationing out the food delivered by Christian Relief Ministries, that there was little or no energy left by the end of the day for actual rebuilding. It felt like she'd been in this limbo for years.

She handed the power cord to eager hands as a young mother in bare feet made her way up the small hill. The woman's milk had dried up right after the quake, probably because it took days for anyone to locate a clean water supply to provide for this many people. Marisol had been walking to the mission compound every week to beg for more formula.

"Please let me help somehow. I'll work for it. I can sweep or pass out food or clear branches." Marisol adjusted her baby in her sling as Megan counted out the cans of formula.

"No, this is a gift and given freely. You have your own children to worry about and your own home to rebuild."

Marisol offered her profuse thanks as well as her regular promises to find a way to repay the mission for their help. Megan wiped the sweat off her forehead. They hadn't even reached the hottest part of the day yet, and she was exhausted.

"Take a drink." Her coworker came up beside her and handed her a bottle of water, which had become one of the mission's most important commodities. "You need your energy."

She hated to take it when there were so many others in the village doing without, but he pressed it into her hands. "Come on. You're not going to be able to help anyone if you don't keep up your health."

Megan couldn't argue with him. Swallowing down her guilt, she tilted her head back and drank greedily.

"Are you expecting any more deliveries from Christian Relief?" he asked.

Megan shook her head. "Not until next week."

"That's what I thought. I wonder who this new guy is then." They watched the truck as it kicked up dust along the dirt road. Several kids ran after it, shouting and hollering in excitement.

Megan didn't care who it was driving once she realized that the truck-bed was piled high with water jugs. Clean, potable water. She rushed ahead, nearly faint from heat and exhaustion as well as joy.

Water. More than enough to last until Christian Relief's next delivery.

She jumped onto the back of the truck when it parked, realizing in an instant she'd have chaos on her hands if she didn't come up with a fair and equitable way to distribute this precious treasure. "Listen up," she called out. "There's enough here for everyone, but we need you to give us room so we know how much we have before we start passing it out."

She made her way to the driver, who had just stepped out of the truck.

"*Muchas gracias, señor*," she began and then stopped when he turned around and mopped his brow with his bandana.

His eyes met hers, and joy surged up in her entire being. She was running before she could even say his name.

"Brad!" She jumped into his arms, and he spun her around with a shout that set all the village children laughing.

She was filthy. Filthy and exhausted and covered in sweat and nearly a month's worth of grime and hard work and backbreaking disappointments.

But he didn't seem to care.

"What are you doing here?" she asked, dizzy when her feet finally found the ground once more.

"What I should have done years ago," he answered, cupping her dirt-caked cheeks with his hands and kissing her right there in front of everybody.

Village boys whooped and hollered, but Brad waved them off with his hand.

When he finally pulled away, they were both breathless. "That's what I came here for." He pointed to the stacked pallets. "That and to deliver this water."

He jumped onto the back of the truck. "All right, listen up." His voice carried over the excitement and chatter below, and even though he spoke with a heavy American accent, his Spanish flowed readily. "We've got another delivery coming the day after tomorrow, so for now it's two gallons per person, and you've got to sign it out with your name and address before you take it home. You littler ones, if you're not going to be able to carry that much with you, I want you to go get an older sibling or parent to come over here and help. And spread the word. There's enough for everyone. Let's start a line right here, and we'll do this in a calm and organized manner."

She still had a hard time believing he was actually here. "Care to lend an old friend a hand?" he asked as he raised her up beside him on the truck-bed.

"Of course I'll help, but you have a lot of explaining to do. You know that, don't you?"

He shrugged and smiled. "What's there to explain? I heard you all needed water out here, and I know how to drive a truck. It was the easiest decision I've made in my entire life."

"Wait, so how long are you going to be here?"

"Long enough to pass out this water at least." He pulled out a clipboard and leaned down toward the young girl who was first in line. "All right. Can you tell me your name and where you live?"

"I'm serious," Megan told him when he straightened back up again. "I haven't heard from you since I left Washington. I think you could give me a slightly longer explanation than that."

"I would have called or emailed," he answered with a grin, "but nothing works yet, and when your brother told me it could be another month or two before you guys get communication with the outside world, I decided that was just too long to wait."

"So you just hopped on a plane?"

"Yup. I just hopped on a plane. Sound like anyone you know?"

She smiled. "How long are you going to stay here?"

"Well, I'm going to deliver this water. I know that much at least. And after that, you and I are overdue to have a very lengthy conversation. Now are you going to help me pass out these jugs, or am I going to have to do all the heavy lifting myself?"

CHAPTER 70

The night was perfectly still, although Megan's ears still rang with the noise and commotion of the day.

Now all she could hear was the faint thudding of Brad's heart as they lay on their backs and she rested with her ear against his chest.

"This view beats Vermont any day of the week." He stretched his arms up behind his head, and Megan nestled a little closer to him. They had been so busy during the day, she had only had a few minutes to scrub down as best as she could and change her clothes before she met him on the little hilltop that overlooked the village.

"Everyone here really loves you," he remarked, breaking their comfortable silence. "It's neat to see the way they respond to you."

She didn't answer. Part of her was still afraid that if she spoke, if she said or did anything unusual, she'd wake up and realize this whole day had been a dream, her subconscious way of worrying over the fact that when she woke up she'd still miss Brad like crazy and still have to find a way to make the mission's limited supplies stretch out until the next relief delivery.

My cup runneth over. How often had she recited that verse with the kids in her class at the school without ever really thinking through what the words meant?

Brad ran his fingers softly through her hair.

She could stay like this forever but figured she should at least try to do something to break the silence. "So catch me up on everything back home. I've gotten exactly one letter from Susannah and Scott, and that's all I've heard from anyone in the States."

"Well, Kitty's home from the hospital. They finally got the pneumonia under control, but she's a lot weaker and she's got her own oxygen supply now at the house, and she uses it most of the time. But her spirits are as high as ever. Susannah told me to tell you that Kitty thinks you're a lot prettier than your brother, and I have to admit I agree."

Even though it was dark, she buried her face in his chest to hide her blush.

"And what else?" he continued. "Susannah's doing fine with the pregnancy. They found out it's going to be a baby girl, and they're going to name her Gloria after Susannah's mom."

"That's sweet. What about your family?" she asked. "How's Grandma Lucy?"

"Sharp as ever. She refused to go back to Seattle for more tests, but from everything I've seen, she's completely back to her normal self, like the dementia never bothered her a day in her life."

"Wow, that's amazing."

"I'll say. She's been praying for you hours a day and for all the relief work going on out here."

"When you go back home, you'll have to tell her how thankful I am." Oops. Why had she mentioned his going home already? There was no reason to jump into such a depressing topic now, not when they'd had such a good first day together already.

He rolled onto his side and faced her. His nose was less than an inch away.

"That's something I wanted to talk to you about." He cleared his throat. Here it was. The part where he told her he was flying back tomorrow. Wouldn't that be her luck?

"I know it would have been best to talk to you about it first, but there wasn't any way to get hold of you. And I knew once I got down here it might be a while before I could call or email anyone back in the States, so I made a decision. I hope you're not mad."

271

Uh-oh. What was he going to tell her?

"I called the director at the boys' home to let him know I'd be coming down here. I told him it might not be a bad idea to start looking for someone to take my place at the school."

"Wait, you're not going back this fall?"

"I didn't want to make any major decisions. Not without talking to you about it first."

"Talking to me about what?"

"About whether you think there's work for me to do here. If there's even the remotest chance God might be calling me to stay."

She sat up, unable to think clearly when his lips were that close to hers.

"You seriously want to stay in Costa Rica long-term?"

"I've been praying about it a lot, yeah. I can teach. I know Spanish. Until the school's up and running again, I figure I can help with all the rebuilding. I've been saving up, so I wouldn't need to raise any official support for a while yet. The only question is whether you think there's work for me to do here and whether you'd like for me to stay."

In the moonlight, his eyes looked so hopeful. So sincere.

"Do you need more time to think about it?" Was that actually fear in his voice?

She leaned down and kissed him. Slowly. Patiently, as if they had all the time in the world.

She pulled away and smiled. "All right. I've thought about it."

"And what did you decide?"

There was only one way she knew of to take that smug grin off his face. She leaned down toward him again. "This is what I decided."

"Can I take that as a yes?" he asked before his lips found hers.

This time, there was no reason to answer.

A NOTE FROM THE AUTHOR

I hope you've enjoyed Megan and Brad's story! If you've read other books in the Sweet Dreams Christian romance series, you might have noticed that I like writing about missionaries, like Scott and Susannah, whose love story is based on my own. If you haven't read their romance yet, you might enjoy *What Dreams May Come.*

You can also read more about Susannah and her sister Kitty in *Dare to Dream Again*, the story of how Susannah's mother and stepfather fell in love while working together one summer at a Vacation Bible School.

Grandma Lucy is also a main character in the Orchard Grove series, which highlights married couples walking through various trials that many believers face.

I'd like to thank the Lord for helping me get this book written and edited (in spite of a three-day power outage that left hundreds of us Alaskans without electricity, water, or heat in the middle of winter). A big thanks to my team of editors, my great cover designer, and my behind-the-scenes miracle-worker Cheri.

My husband remains my biggest encourager. I know I couldn't write these stories if I hadn't experienced a love as strong as his firsthand.

Thanks also to everyone who reads my novels! When you buy an Alana Terry book, you are supporting a ministry that God is using in tremendous ways. Thanks to your continued readership, we've been able to raise over fifteen thousand dollars to assist refugees through Liberty in North Korea's underground railroad.

By reading these novels, you are truly changing the world!

Jump into your next Alana Terry book at www.alanaterry.com.

Made in the USA
Columbia, SC
31 August 2019